PINK EYE

TOM NORTON

ABSURD PRESS

ISBN: 9780645848892

Publisher: ABSURD PRESS

1

PARKES, NEW SOUTH WALES

SHIT. Almost midnight. He was going to be late. Albert gripped the steering wheel as the station wagon bounced along the dirt road. Couldn't this piece of junk go faster? Ahead, the giant radio telescope towered out of the darkness. Albert glanced up through his windscreen at the night sky. The light from those stars had taken years to arrive. Being a couple of minutes late wouldn't affect anything. Besides, the boss had probably already left.

His headlights flashed over a mob of sleepy kangaroos. One drowsy marsupial turned its head, watching his car judder across potholes. Lucky roos. They eat grass, jump around, make babies and have zero existential worries about being alone in the universe.

His car sped into the observatory car park and skidded to a stop. The glowing clock on his dashboard read just after twelve. Only a few minutes late. A grin spread across his bearded face. The master of the roads and the stars.

Flicking on the light, he snatched his backpack off the passenger seat and caught sight of his bloodshot eyes in the rear-vision mirror. They looked worse than tired; his eyes were pink and fractured like eggshells. His dad's had been like this before anyone knew he was sick. God, Albert could still hear, and smell,

I

his dad's words as they camped out in their backyard. Little Albert staring into his telescope with his old man hunched over, whispering about the constellations. Those nights, his dad's breath had smelt of burnt herbs, a scent Albert learnt was his father's self-medicating act of defiance. Albert blinked at his red eyes in the mirror. Just get through tonight. It'll be okay. He brushed down his dark, messy curls with his fingers to appear normal.

Three kangaroos, chewing grass at the edge of the car park popped up their heads as he slammed the car door. His sneakers crunched across the gravel. Both pride and exhaustion filled his heart as the huge white dish towered above him like a massive ear to the stars.

Galaxies, supernovas and the possibility of something being out there were Albert's passions, but being enthusiastic about data entry required effort. For the last few months he'd been yearning for a transfer to day shifts. If only. Regular sleep sounded so seductive, so out of reach, and yet beautiful. It was a mythical creature. He desired that magic slumber beast so much, he would willingly consent to it dragging him into his bedroom and ravishing him. After tonight's shift, he'd face plant into his pillow and try to sleep for the entire weekend.

He slapped his ID pass against the access panel and the glass doors slid open. "Kaz?" he called, praying for zero response. "You still here?"

The air conditioner whirred in the empty office.

He stopped holding his breath. "Kaz?"

The fluorescent lights above the open-plan cubicles hummed. Brilliant. This was perfect. He almost skipped towards his office. It was just him and the stars.

"Doctor Manning!" a woman's voice boomed in a battle cry. A tall woman came striding between the desks like a Valkyrie in suit and tie. "We need to talk."

Albert swallowed. His stomach twisted in a tense knot. Why Kaz dressed formally in rural Australia he could never understand.

Her blonde hair was tied back so tight it stretched her face and her square jawline was brick hard.

Her cold eyes flicked over him as she said, "Whatever you're wearing, it's breaking office policy." Her lips puckered into a sneer. "Are you supposed to be an astrophysicist or a hobo?"

Albert's body ached from tiredness. He glanced down at his old jeans and t-shirt. "At this hour, Kaz, no one cares."

"Doctor Manning, this isn't university. Your lazy PhD days are over." She struck her hands against her hips. "Parkes Observatory is the most significant observatory in our great nation. Protocol can not to be ignored." On each side of her jaw, muscles pulsed.

Albert stood more upright, readying to defend himself.

She continued, "I will not have you tarnishing our reputation with your layabout attitude."

"Kaz, I'm not lazy." He felt exhausted. "Admittedly, my clothing might not be to your taste, but my entries are on point and accurate. I do this job exceedingly well."

Her eyes flared. Angry. If she even slightly agreed, she didn't show it. "Project Big Ear requires lots of responsibility. Show it in your attire." Her lips compressed. "Turning up late is unacceptable. This is the second time—"

"I'm only five min—"

"Don't interrupt." She held up her hand as if she were a traffic cop. "While some might be kind enough to suggest your work is acceptable, you must arrive on time and well groomed." She took a breath and glanced him up and down. "Dressing like a loser is a distasteful reflection of our institute's values. This your first official warning."

He nodded. Thank the universe this was his last shift for the week.

"Unless, of course," – she leaned down close to his face and hissed – "you can make it worth my while."

Albert looked at her, confused. Was she? No, she couldn't.

"Kaz..." he began, "you're very lovely, but I don't think of you that way."

"No, you twit." Her eyes shot wide. "I know some people find you" – her eyes scrutinized his face – "attractive, for a nerd. But I do not." She huffed and glanced around the empty office before whispering, "Give me ten per cent of your pay each week and your warning disappears."

Albert stepped back, feeling off balance.

"Plus" – she smiled – "I'll ensure your employment in our great facility is always secure."

She was too much.

"No." He forced himself to stare into her eyes. "That won't be happening." If he paid her, he'd only have enough for rent and nothing else.

"Okay, Manning." She plastered on her smile. "But one more warning and you're out on that threadbare arse." She spun on her heels and strode towards the main doors, calling behind her, "Now remember: shoot for the stars."

Albert slumped into his chair. Above him, data streamed across screens displaying the incoming universe. On the monitor directly in front of him, Big Kaz had stuck a pink Post-it-Note: *First Warning!*

He peeled it off. She was a jerk. No way did he deserve a warning. Sure, he dressed casually, but his clothing wasn't a representation of his work. He'd still be brilliant in his underpants. The universe was messy, and so was he. Carl Sagan would never have put up with this.

Albert began to punch in the coordinates for the night's observations. His fingers smashed the keyboard with such determination as he hoped each hit would push the thought of Kaz's angry face further away. For the last five years he'd enthusiastically, painstakingly and, even under the duress of hangovers, doggedly finished his doctorate with extreme accuracy, at times falling asleep face down in his notes before being ejected from libraries by apologetic librarians at closing time. Tonight's reporting would be even more on point. The planets inside the Pictor constellation would be monitored with gusto.

The motors controlling the massive telescope hummed to life. Their sound calmed his mind as the thousand-tonne parabolic dish above him tilted ever so slightly to focus on another tiny sector of the sky. Soon information from the sector began streaming in, lighting the screens with tiny blips of information from the region's star and planets. His fingers flew across the keyboard, entering quick and brief comments about the numbers being recorded, as though he were the most important data-entry person in the world. He was the prime minister of data entry.

Sometimes he likened this job of pointing Project Big Ear at a patch of sky to sitting in a dark movie theatre and waiting for a film to begin. The movie might start in five years, but it probably wouldn't. More likely, it would start five hundred years after he was dead. What's more, in this particular cinema, no one knew in which direction the screen was. Come to think of it, no one knew whether it was a cinema at all. Rather, he was just sitting in some dark room that smelt of stale popcorn, unwashed fabric and a hint of vomit, waiting for something to happen.

An hour later, he leaned back from the keyboard, stretched and yawned. Numbers continued to stream. Nothing seemed to be happening. He stood up to take a toilet break when every monitor flashed like a high-wattage Christmas tree.

"Oh my god!" His voice echoed around the empty offices. Data exploded across the screens. Fantastic! But he had to be sure. Did the signal have the intense noise of a supernova? No. Good. Was this star in the Pictor constellation stable? Yes. No comets were scheduled to pass through his field of observation, no asteroids were in the path. And the signal was much more controlled than the static he'd receive from random space objects.

It had to be coming from one of the planets he was monitoring.

He glanced at the black-and-white polarisation charts. The signal appeared as a horizontal straight black line surrounded by static; a narrow band of extreme frequency that was too long to be a fast radio burst, so it wasn't from a mobile phone or a microwave oven, which had caused problems in the past. This signal was the real deal.

He checked the location of the galaxy and took a deep breath. It might be coming from planet HD 40307 g, right inside the Goldilocks zone – not too hot and not too cold, perfect for life.

"This could be big."

Albert dropped into his seat and leaned forward, scanning the data stream. The signal had lasted exactly seventy-two seconds. He stared at the screen, waiting for something more to happen.

The screens blinked silently.

Why seventy-two seconds? Seventy-two was half a gross or six dozen. Sixty in duodecimal. It was the sum of four consecutive primes, as well as the sum of six consecutive primes. Seventy-two was a pronic number, which was the product of two consecutive numbers, in this case eight and nine.

While his mind was flooding with number theories, his bladder was under enough pressure to rupture. But if he did a toilet dash now the screen would surely light up again. This was too huge. Squirming in his chair, squeezing himself tight, he recalculated combinations of the seventy-two-second problem. He was nearly going to burst before he grabbed an empty water bottle off his desk, unzipped his jeans and relieved himself.

Looking from the warm yellow liquid to the screens, the excitement passed. Still nothing. He should probably start informing people; Big Kaz would be over the moon. No doubt she'd receive an award. The thought of her receiving all the credit made his skin crawl. Screw Kaz. If this was actual proof of first contact, he should be awarded a professorship.

Albert leaned forward to examine the recorded waveform. He zoomed in on it. The signal was an incomprehensible jumble of squiggles, a big spaghetti mess. Bloody hell, the most important day in Earth's history, when an alien race possibly makes contact and their message makes as much sense as a talking goat.

He ran the recording through a series of filters to remove the extraneous noise and the signal stretched out in a clearer waveform. Regularities within the frequencies began to take form. Slowly, he recognised the patterns. They were using a form of frequency modulation, and parts of the code were repeating at the beginning and end. Coding and data analysis were his passions; his exhaustion evaporated as his brain kicked into a rhythm.

By the end of his shift, Albert had formed a theory about the repeating pattern: it could mean only one thing. He copied the recording to his laptop, buried the data from it in his work folders, and slapped a Post-it Note on his boss' desk.

Nothing to report. Quiet night.

———

For two days Albert hunched over the computer in his bedroom, fingers tapping across the keyboard; empty mugs teetering on every remaining surface of the desk and, finally an hour before he was due back for his Monday night shift, he'd finished building the signal convertor program. Bathed in blue light from his monitor with his head buzzing from caffeine and lack of sleep, Albert pushed up his glasses. The small green icon sat on the screen, beckoning him. He stared at it for a full ten minutes, as if frozen. This could change the world. It could change everything. He breathed in and out. Then his wrist slid the mouse over the little green box and he clicked.

On the screen, a green creature stared back as though it was checking the camera, and then formed a smile of sharp teeth. It looked like a cross between a human and the ugliest toad Albert had ever seen. It had a mop of stringy hair, the colour of moss, and slime dripping down its face as though it was sweating gloop. A silver robe hung from its body and its long hands shone wetly.

"Hello," it intoned. "My name is Blixitor. I am a representative of the Gatogrosian Council, a group of unified civilisations in the known universe."

Albert started jotting down details.

"The message we sent was very simple. We estimated it would take a species at your level of evolution no more than twenty minutes to decode."

Well, Albert thought, I'll be editing out that part.

"We learnt your language through your radio broadcasts. We very much enjoyed the jazz. Louis Armstrong is quite the hepcat."

Albert did a quick calculation. It would've taken forty-two years for Earth's radio signals to reach their planet and, if Blixitor returned a broadcast straight away, it would've taken another forty-two for his message to arrive. The alien was listening to Louis' trumpet wails from the 1930s.

Blixitor continued. "We would like to offer your planet something that will change your lives forever. For the better, of course. Our next transmission will be much longer and contain very important details. Show it directly to your leaders. We will broadcast again in exactly three Earth days."

Albert checked the clock on his phone. Tonight, he didn't want to be late.

———

The wagon skidded into the gravel car park. Albert slammed the car door and ran towards the observatory.

"Bit early, aren't you?" Big Kaz stood in the hallway, dressed in a suit and tie, blocking the way to Albert's office.

"I came in early to make up the time."

Her cold eyes ran him up and down, her lips twitched. Albert glanced down at himself and winced. Damn. These were the same jeans and t-shirt he'd worn on Friday's shift and he hadn't had time to shower.

"You look appalling" – she winced with her nose wrinkling at his body odour – "Go home and clean yourself up."

"I'm sorry, Kaz. I understand this isn't appropriate."

She glared at him. The muscles in her square jaw pulsing.

Albert realised if she stopped him, he would miss the broadcast. He decided to appeal to her compassion, if it existed. "Kaz, I don't own anything else. And honestly, I'm going to buy some new clothes when I get paid."

Her eyes narrowed and her lips smiled, thinly. "This will be your last warning, Doctor Manning. You're going to have to leave."

"No. I can't." Albert looked sideways to his office, trying to control his anxiousness. "Tonight's reports will be on your desk in the morning," he lied again. "I promise. And I'll never turn up to work like this again. Everything will be perfect."

"I've given you too many chances," Kaz huffed. "Unless, of course, we can come to some sort of agreement."

And there it was, he thought. He did a quick calculation. "Alright," he said. "Ten percent of my daily pay rounded to the nearest hundred."

"Very well." She grinned and stepped aside. "I want the report from tonight on my desk before you leave."

"It will be." He smiled. Ten per cent of his daily pay was thirty dollars, and that, rounded to the nearest hundred, was zero. "Things are going to be much different from now on. Trust me."

"Yes, I believe our working relationship has already improved." She shook her car keys and marched towards the doors. "Now remember, shoot for the stars."

Albert slipped eagerly into his chair under the bank of screens and breathed deep before carefully punching in the coordinates for the Pictor constellation. The dish's motors hummed to life, moving it slowly into position. He glanced at his monitor, at the data streaming in from outer space. It was being recorded, but he uploaded his decoding program to convert any incoming signal on the fly.

Everything was quiet, nothing unusual was going on yet. On his desk he noticed the water bottle filled with his piss from the other night. Kaz had stuck a note to it: *No juice near the equipment.* No time for that now, this was history in the making.

He took a deep breath, feeling doubt creep into his mind. His hands hung poised over the keyboard. This next step could get him into a little trouble. The world had to be informed and he definitely wanted to be the one telling them, but some might think he had no right. He straightened his back, trying to find his confidence. Doing this was breaking the rules.

Screw the rules, he thought. Screw Kaz. He was going to change the world.

Quickly, he logged on to every social media account he had and set up multiple live streams, each page with the same title – "First Contact with Aliens Tonight". He summarised his last few days of work, posted the first decoded video as proof and added a large countdown timer to display when the broadcast would begin, assuming the aliens wouldn't be late.

Remember to breathe. Forcing himself to exhale, he watched the screen. Slowly, the decoded video's view count rose. In a just few minutes, three people had watched.

The alien's voice echoed through his head: "Show it directly to your leaders." Was this the right thing to do? His stomach bubbled as if inside it contained a thick soup of anxiety. If he had shown this to Kaz, whatever the outcome, he would've felt much worse. He closed his eyes, trying to calm his brain. Whatever Blixitor had to say, the whole human race would understand. After all, we are all equal. And who the hell are our leaders? When he opened his eyes, the view count had risen to thirteen. Double figures.

As more and more people watched, Albert scrolled down to the comments. *If tonight is first contact,* someone wrote, *what was that video posted? Pre-emptive contact?* They added a laughing emoji.

How many prequels are there?

Albert pressed his lips together and pushed up his glasses.

Blood began heating his face. Ignore them, he thought. There will always be haters.

The view count clicked above the hundreds, and others said, *This is fake news. The video is a hoax.*

Albert's fingers flew across the keyboard with fury. This would not do at all. After explaining who he was, he smashed the keys with his IP address to prove his location. He forced his eyes away from the computer, up at the quiet equipment monitoring the Pictor constellation. Soon everything would light up like a rave party. Online, questions about his authenticity began to dissolve and the tight unease in his gut loosened. He felt proud that people knew he was broadcasting from Parkes Observatory. He wasn't some crazy person, but a proper scientist who sat in the dark waiting for aliens to speak.

Five minutes before the broadcast was due to start, Albert adjusted his glasses and attempted to flatten his curly hair before turning on the webcam. "Hello, everyone," he said in an unfortunately squeaky voice. "Today, we are going to make history." He held up his fist. "Woo!"

You look awful, someone commented in the feed. *Are you sick?*

I think he's cute. But yeah... definitely unwell.

Albert looked at the tiny video portrait of his face in the top corner of the screen and nodded in agreement. He did look terrible. His glasses exacerbated the dark rings under his eyes. His black curly hair stood at crazy angles and he hadn't shaved. "Sorry, I haven't slept for a couple of days," he explained. "I've been decoding the other video."

I bet he's on drugs, another commented.

"Honestly, I'm just tired."

That's denial. He's probably on meth.

"No, I'm not. It's coffee."

Albert's eyes went wide, seeing the number of streamers had climbed into the hundreds of thousands. Nervousness rushed through him. Not since Parkes Observatory broadcast the moon landing had this many people taken notice. His breath became short and he forced himself to smile into the webcam. Make a good impression, he thought. This was going viral.

Admit it. You're off your head, aren't you?

"No!"

Oh look. It's starting.

The video screen in front of Albert flashed white. Albert's watching face sat in the top corner of the feed.

"This is it," said Albert, using a calm, soft voice for the audience of the world. He imagined himself narrating a documentary. "This is first contact. History is about to be made."

On the screen, an animation of lots of strange logos flew past to form a circle surrounded by stars.

Albert continued, "That appears to be a symbol of the Gatogrosian Council. Next, I assume we will see their representative, Blixitor."

Shut up, Albert! You're ruining it!

Blixitor appeared on screen. The smiling alien toad wearing a silver robe reminded Albert of a sweaty monk. Slime shimmered on its skin. Its green hair hung limp. Stretching out its long glistening hands, it said, "Greetings from the unified planets of the Gatogrosian Council."

God, he's an ugly bastard, came a comment. *If that thing landed in my backyard, I'd take its head off with a shovel.*

"Thank you for this opportunity," Blixitor continued. "And for allowing me to talk directly with your leader. It is a great honour."

Albert felt himself blushing slightly with pride. He was making this happen. The greatest moment Earth had known. This was huge. He would definitely get an award.

I never voted for Albert. He's not my leader. He's a junky.

All hail Emperor Albert... Drug head.

Blixitor continued, "You're probably wondering why we decided to contact you."

No, we're not. We wanna know where you get your hair done. The worst barber in the universe. Zero stars.

"I am head of the Gatogrosian division of xenopologists. Our task is to study cultures on different planets. We assess them, determine their level of evolution and offer our help."

At this point, the phone on Albert's desk began to ring. Albert paused the video stream. Blixitor's green face stopped, frozen. In the top corner of the screen, Albert watched himself say, "Don't worry, everyone. The video is still recording. We won't miss anything. I just have to take this." As his phone rang, the world watched. "Hello?"

"What the hell do you think you're doing?" yelled Big Kaz.

"Um, Kaz. Is there a problem?"

"Don't play games with me. Turn off that broadcast immediately."

"But..."

Our great leader is getting totally owned.

"Turn it off!" Kaz shouted.

Hang up on her, Albert.

"End it!" screamed his boss. "NOW!"

Albert looked at the paused screen with the frozen image of Blixitor's head and his own nervous face in the top corner. This was his moment, his chance to change the world. There would never be another. "Sorry." He hung up and pressed play.

"The Gatogrosians have no plans to visit Earth," Blixitor said. "Our system is too far away. It would take at least a thousand years before we arrived."

It sounds like Blixie's government has cut his funding.

Same story, different planet.

He should ask Emperor Albert for some money.

"But," continued Blixitor, "we have developed a form of wormhole communication technology. If you build this, we can communicate and send information back and forth at great distances instantaneously. We will be able to speak directly with each other in real-time."

Awesome. A Universe Wide Web.

Oh great! We're going to be watching Blixie's cat videos.

"We would like to offer your planet this extremely advanced technology. This will improve your people's lives. It has the potential to change your world beyond your imagination for the betterment of all."

The phone rang again, and Albert unplugged it. Then the mobile phone in his pocket started vibrating. He threw it across the room.

Albert took a deep breath and imagined people all over planet Earth watching on TVs, computers, phones or whatever screen they had, leaning forward.

"But in exchange for this information, Gatogrosians wish to study humans in their natural habitats without their knowledge. They are not to know they are being watched or even be aware of our existence. These humans must not know," it repeated. "They must not know of our existence. All aspects of this negotiation depend on this. The only ones who can know are a small group of world leaders. The general population must not know about us for this to succeed."

"Oops," said Albert.

A bit late for that now, isn't it?

I bet Emperor Albert feels like a goose.

Albert's mobile continued to vibrate from across the room.

"As a sign of trust and a show of our respect," Blixitor said, "I will now stream some blueprints and codes for the advanced technology that will allow us to communicate directly."

At this point, Blixitor disappeared, and the screen went black. Random codes and diagrams started firing across the monitor.

"Holy shit!" yelled Albert in the corner of the screen. He leaned forwards, watching. I'm going to be famous, he thought, I'm going to win the Nobel Prize. Stick that up your arse, Big Kaz.

The door to his office flung open. Albert's eyes went wide as several federal police officers burst into the room, pointing handguns.

"Get away from the computer!" an officer shouted.

Another grabbed him by the collar. Albert squealed and as

they shoved him backwards from the desk, his legs kicked out and booted the bottle of yellow wee. He fell and the bottle flew up, spinning slowly above him like a satellite before they both crashed to the floor. The bottle pooled in a puddle near his head as a knee went into his back and handcuffs clicked tight around his wrists.

2

TWO YEARS LATER

BOBBY TUCKER GLANCED around the classroom, wide-eyed and worried. Dial down the paranoia, he thought. No one is looking. Every other student faced the front with rapt attention, as if their new teacher held the gift for imparting great wisdom. He leaned down close to his desk, cupped a hand over his mouth and sniffed. Damn. That herb smell was hanging around like a bad fart. Should never have vaped pot during the break. Physics was gonna cook the brain.

Ms Jacobs paced at the front, before the rows of desks like an evangelical preacher with a pixie haircut. "We're taking a giant leap today," she said.

He watched her beautiful lips move.

"We're talking about space."

My head is in outer space, he thought, rubbing his red-rimmed eyes. Mental note: Stop getting stoned at lunch. It might mess up university next year.

His teacher was explaining how the Earth orbited the sun at thirty kilometres per second. If you asked Bobby, the world wasn't moving fast enough; another six months of St Helens High would destroy him. But moving to Hobart University, that'd be next level. No parents, no rules, just parties.

"And the sun is orbiting the centre of the Milky Way," Ms Jacobs said, "at two hundred and thirty kilometres per second."

No wonder I feel dizzy. He rubbed his hands over his black spikey hair, trying to wake up.

Ms Jacobs flicked on the interactive whiteboard. A photo of a massive radio telescope popped up. Bobby leaned forward in his chair, trying to appear interested like everyone else. Don't draw attention. Just act straight, like another regular kid in class. He nodded as Ms Jacobs spoke. With her slender hand pointing out different parts of the dish, she was ridiculously sexy for an old girl. She must be at least thirty.

Ms Jacobs asked, "Can someone tell me what electromagnetism is?"

Bobby lowered his head, pretending to read his textbook to avoid her gaze.

His best friend, Chook, wearing the serene smile of the relaxed stoner, leaned over near Bobby's ear and whispered, "I'm pretty sure you're receiving some electromagnetic attraction from Kitty."

Bobby glanced over and noticed Kitty's legs first, bare and crossed towards him. Why was she was staring at him? He attempted to sit more upright. Act straight, he told himself again. Be confident, like a player. Kitty was good-looking – not in the way Ms Jacobs was, because his teacher owned beauty that was out of this world, but Kitty also ranked high on the hotness scale: blue hair, nose ring and now the cutest grin. Bobby smiled back and gave her an awkward little wave. As soon as he did, he could've slapped himself for being so lame. Waving was diabolically *un*-player like. Kitty smiled and looked away. Bobby felt his face burning.

"Hey, Tucker," someone said from behind.

Bobby looked around to see Dave, Kitty's boyfriend. The freakishly massive boy glared at him with a deep frown between his eyes. Dave flipped up his middle finger. Bobby quickly turned back and stared at his desk. Great, now he had that giant douche giving him grief. Acting normal, he thought, complete fail.

Chook muffled his giggles.

"Mister Adams." Ms Jacobs zeroed in on Chook. "Would you mind telling us what's so funny? Or perhaps you could share your thoughts on the speed of radio waves through space."

"I guess everything is about timing." Chook laughed stupidly, his ginger head nodding. "Bobby and I" – he pointed – "were just discussing how fast things move when you're spaced."

Bobby groaned. The class turned their eyes on him like hungry vultures expecting a meal of embarrassing entertainment. Bobby wanted to climb under his desk. Why did Chook have to throw him under the bus?

"Mister Tucker, care to elaborate?"

He could feel himself sinking further into his chair, so he took a deep breath, straightened himself upright and said, "Of course. Not a problem. What Chook means is that radio waves are a type of electromagnetic radiation that travel at the speed of light." He grinned. "So their timing has to be mega quick."

"And what is the speed of light?"

"Just under 300 thousand kilometres a second."

Ms Jacobs laughed out a single honk noise and said, "Nice save, Mister Tucker."

The class grumbled, disappointed. Bobby felt a warm flush on his cheeks. Ms Jacobs gave him a quick smile and turned back to her whiteboard, pointing at the radio telescope. Bobby watched. Sure, Ms Jacobs had a weird laugh, but no one was perfect.

She said, "Electromagnetic radiation is made of an elementary particle called a photon. And, as Bobby has stated, these travel at the speed of light."

His heart fluttered. Maybe he truly was in love with Ms Jacobs. She might be the one. Perhaps it could work, despite their age difference. He could still feel Kitty's eyes on him, but ignored her, looking directly at Ms Jacobs' beautiful body. A plan formed in his head. He would be the best student she'd ever had. He would win her favour and then, when he finished year twelve, they'd go out on a sexy date.

A tightly folded up note landed on his desk. Bobby glanced back in the direction it had come and Kitty nodded with a wink. Bobby swallowed down his rising discomfort. Had Dave seen her do that? Her little letter sat on his desk waiting like an unopened birthday present.

Ms Jacobs' phoned dinged.

"No phones in class, Miss," Dave called from the back of the room. The class muffled their sniggers.

"Chill out, Dave," Bobby said.

"I'll smash your face, Tucker."

"Dave." Kitty rolled her eyes. "Don't be a dick."

Bobby's head dropped, regretting having opened his mouth. He really should think first.

Ms Jacobs stared pointedly at them before she continued. "I've just received some very important information."

With the class focused on her, Bobby began to unfold Kitty's note. Feather scraped his stomach. Did Kitty like him? God, she was hot. Scribbled in pencil the note read: *Stay the fuck away from me and my brother.* He looked back and she was glaring. No smile. The feathers in his stomach turned into knives.

Ms Jacobs continued, "Tell your parents and everyone you know that there is a compulsory meeting tonight at the town hall."

Bobby wished his seat would swallow him.

"I can't go," Dave called out. "We've got footy training."

"David, it'll be cancelled."

"Not likely. The grand final's on this weekend."

"David, I promise you, training won't be on. Everyone must attend this meeting."

Dave huffed. Bobby kept his eyes straight ahead. He didn't want to say anything else to piss off Dave or Kitty.

Chook asked, "Is the meeting about tourists and the upcoming fishing season?"

"I don't think so," Ms Jacobs said. "That wouldn't be compulsory."

"What's it about then?" Kitty asked.

"I'm not sure." Ms Jacobs frowned at her phone. "The government is organising it and tonight's announcement will affect you all."

The school's bell started to ring. Bobby shoved his books into his bag. He couldn't wait to get outside. The room felt hot.

"Before you go," Ms Jacobs said to everyone, "your home-work is to research whether anything can travel faster than light. And tell me why or why not."

The class erupted into chatter as they all grabbed their bags to leave.

"See you at the meeting," Ms Jacobs called above the noise.

That night, as Bobby followed his mum and her boyfriend through the doors of the town hall, a smiling woman in a suit stopped them. "I'm Sally. Welcome to the meeting. Before you can come in" – she held out a clipboard and a pen – "you'll need to sign this non-disclosure agreement."

"Why do I need to sign an NDA?" Bobby heard the anger in his mum voice as he wandered past.

"I know this isn't normal procedure for the government to engage the community," Sally said, "but information booths are inside if you have any questions." She glanced at Bobby walking away. "Are you that boy's guardian? You'll have to sign for him too."

Intense chatter filled the room and Bobby was amazed at how many people were inside. Lots of people were crowded around the info tables set up around the hall. Immediately, Bobby scanned the faces for Chook. The ginger ninja had to be somewhere. Kitty caught his eye and nodded back. Quickly, he looked at his shoes as awkward heat flushed his face. He'd been stupid. She never liked him. Thankfully, Dave was nowhere in sight.

Families kept shuffling through the doors. Everyone's so dressed up, he thought. His mum wore her favourite yellow dress; their neighbour, Old Bill, had ironed his shirt; and the other fishermen even wore shoes. This meeting must be more important than the bush dance. Bobby was glad he'd worn his favourite t-shirt.

Behind him, Bill said to his mum, "The tides are changing."

"It would seem they are." His mum sounded annoyed.

"And right now the fishing would be deadly. But we're trapped in this government bullshit."

Mayor Brown stood on stage smiling and waiting for everyone to sit. She was flanked by three swanky people, two in suits and one in a military uniform. More government folks, Bobby assumed. At the back of the room he spotted Ms Jacobs behind a table with a sign that read, "Buy a space cake and support St Helens High Science." God, he'd love to squeeze a couple of her cupcakes. Trying to appear taller, he adjusted his spikey hair and strutted through the crowd. Tonight Ms Jacobs looked even hotter than at school with her slim-fitting dress and perfect pixie hair.

"I like your t-shirt," she said.

He glanced down at his favourite meme shirt, a screenshot of Emperor Albert, the idiot scientist who two years ago had failed to hoax the world into believing in aliens. Underneath the image was the word, "Oops!"

Ms Jacobs smiled. "I think you'll find it's very appropriate tonight." Before he could ask why, she continued, "Are those your parents?"

"G'day," said his mum's boyfriend, coming up behind him and shaking Ms Jacobs' hand. "I'm Simon and this is..." He turned to Bobby's mum.

"Doctor Cinnamon Tucker," his mum finished.

"I'm Grace Jacobs, Bobby's science teacher." She smiled.

Grace. Bobby repeated her name in his mind. It was perfect.

"I heard you recently transferred here," his mum said. "How are you finding life in St Helens?"

"You mean honestly?" She paused and smiled. "Everyone has been lovely."

"Has Cinn's little man been causing you trouble?" Simon touched Grace's arm. "I hope so."

Grace honked out a laugh and Simon also laughed, but way too loudly.

Oh god, Bobby thought, feeling himself burning. Simon was totally flirting with her. The guy was a douche. Bobby edged out of the conversation and, thankfully, on the other side of the room, he spotted Chook sitting in a chair by himself.

As Bobby stepped close Chook looked up at him, his eyes wide and rimmed with pink. "This is really weird."

"This?" Bobby shrugged. "A boring town meeting?"

Chook glanced nervously around the room. "I don't think so." He spoke in a soft voice, "Look around and tell me what you see."

Bobby scanned the gathered faces. They all seemed happy. Their lives were so simple, he thought. Simple and boring. University was going to be awesome.

"There's zero strange going on. I wish something was. It'd be way more interesting."

"What about on the balconies?"

Bobby glanced up. The two old balconies with their wooden balustrades that ran along the sides looked even more boring than the meeting. "You're totally stoned, aren't you?"

"No." Chook looked away. "Well, maybe a little, but it's more than that."

Bobby winked. "How 'bout we duck out so I can get toasted too? Then we'll talk weird."

They stepped through a side door into the night. The distant rumble of the surf mixed with the hubbub from inside. Long grass brushed Bobby's legs as they crossed a paddock filled with cars, searching for a quiet spot.

He smiled at Chook. "So, think I've got a chance with her?"

"Sure. Why not?" Chook glanced back at the hall. "Kitty couldn't stop gawking at you in science."

"No, bro. I mean Ms Jacobs."

Chook stopped and regarded him. "Seriously?"

Bobby grinned and continued walking.

"Oi, Tucker!" someone shouted.

The boys spun. Bobby knew that voice. Feeling nervous, he scanned the dark field teeming with families hurrying to the hall, except for Dave, who was striding towards them. Shit. Not now. Was this about Kitty's note? The massive boy weaved through the parked cars.

"Let's leg it," Chook whispered, looking nervously at the hall. "We don't want to create a scene. Not with what's going on in there."

"It'll be cool." Bobby rubbed his hands over his spikey hair to try to make himself more alert. "I'm gonna set him right."

As Dave got closer, Chook edged away. Dave stood a foot taller than Bobby – with his footballer's physique, he was bigger than most adults. "We have a problem." Dave stared down and poked his finger into Bobby's chest. "I saw the stupid wave you gave Kitty."

"The wave?" Bobby almost laughed, but took a deep breath to force down his fear. At least Dave didn't know about her note. "But waving, it's just so friendly." He could feel himself tensing up, adrenaline kicking in. "I wave at everyone. Don't I, Chook?"

"You sure do." Chook shrugged and glanced away. "Hey, look, there are some people." He began waving at a family passing. "Hello. Just waving at you. Nice to see you."

The parents frowned and took the hands of their children and picked up their pace.

Bobby waved at them as well. "Hey there, how you doing?"

He nudged Dave. "Aren't you going to wave? It's nice being friendly."

Dave leaned in near Bobby's face. "Don't go near her. Stay away."

"That'll be difficult," said Chook, still waving. "We see her brother, Baz, all the time."

Bobby had to stop himself from saying, shut up, Chook.

Dave sneered. "I don't give a shit." Strands of facial hair poked out of Dave's chin as he thrust his face close to Bobby's. "Stay away from Kitty."

Dave turned and strode off. Bobby sighed with relief. What the fuck was everyone's' problem? Stay away from this person. Stay away from that one. He needed a list of people that he could talk to.

At the edge of the field, the night surrounded them and Chook pulled out a small black box with a glowing green light. "Well," he said, handing it to Bobby, "you certainly set Dave right."

"Whatever," Bobby said, feeling his anger bubble in his chest. "The guy is a prick." A small bud of marijuana rattled inside Chook's vaporiser. Bobby put the pipe to his lips, pressed a button and sucked in a lungful of warm pot-scented air. For a few seconds, he held his breath and blew out. As he took another long drag, he felt his brain begin to relax. The cogs started unclicking. The tension with Dave evaporated more with each exhale. "So did you ask Baz out when you picked up the weed?"

Chook glared at him. "Just because he's the only other gay in town doesn't mean I'm keen."

"There's always Martin at the library. He seems *very* nice."

"Shut up, dickhead," Chook said, looking back at the hall.

Bobby liked how from here the building seemed to glow and the chatter could still be heard. Tonight, the sky was filled with so many stars.

"Listen," Chook said, "something is seriously wrong in that hall. I can't explain because it's far too weird, even for me, but you need to stay cool when we go back in. No freaking out. If they catch us. We. Will. Be. Fucked. And not in the good way."

Bobby looked at the seriousness in Chook's eyes. He was sprouting some spectrum-level paranoia. Bobby was starting to feel worried about his friend. This wasn't like him. "Who is going to catch us, bro?"

"You won't believe me. It sounds too batshit crazy."

"Try me. I'm a good listener."

"God, I wouldn't believe me."

"Okay then," Bobby said gently, feeling very concerned about Chook. Maybe they both should lay off the pot for a while. He looked at the vaporiser and took one last puff. "Let's do this."

The boys stood at the back of the hall; everyone else was seated facing the stage. There were almost no seats left, except for two at the front.

Chook whispered, "Now don't wig out, but tell me what you see."

Bobby gazed around the room at the families and fishermen sat in their plastic seats, chatting. He looked up on the side balconies and his heart thumped. Soldiers stood in a line, armed and ready. Bobby felt fear rising in his throat. The soldiers appeared almost transparent. Their bodies and guns were a slight shade of pink, but see-through as if they were holograms. Four soldiers stood positioned on either side of the room.

"What the hell?"

"I know," Chook hissed. "Keep your voice down."

Bobby whispered, "They've got machine guns." He glanced sideways at the glowing pink soldiers, trying to take in their appearance without directly looking at them. The guns seemed fragile, as if they were made of pink glass. Two little girls played chasings beneath the balcony, and the soldier paid no attention to the kids, watching the crowd instead. Bobby realised, looking around the room, that no one seemed to give a shit about the soldiers – as if they couldn't see them at all. Was he imagining this? Did Chook slip something trippy into the pot? "Chook, you can see them too, right?"

"I think the pot lets us see them."

Bobby relaxed a little. "So they're invisible?"

"Yes, dickhead."

Bobby peered intently at one of the soldiers, trying to figure out how their invisibility worked. Was it some kind of special paint? "This is serious. We should tell someone."

Chook raised his ginger eyebrow. "Be my guest. Tell your mum."

Bobby looked around and saw Mayor Brown chatting with the two suits and the military lady. Paranoia began to knock on the door to his brain. If the mayor was talking to the military woman, then she probably already knew about the soldiers. Clearly, none of them needed telling. "Okay," he said, "we need to act ultra-cool and not say anything to anyone."

The two of them crept slowly down the aisle between the rows of chairs, trying to appear normal. Two fishermen snickered as they snuck past, one saying, "You lads look cooked." Bobby did his best to keep his eyes straight ahead on the remaining two seats in the front row next to Old Bill.

As Bobby and Chook sat, the mayor took to the stage.

"Hello, everyone." The microphone crackled. "Welcome to our first town meeting." Behind her, on the largest TV screen Bobby had ever seen, one word flickered across it. *Opportunity*.

"I have a very special announcement for you all," Mayor Brown said, smiling with lots of teeth. "The government has chosen our wonderful little town to test some new technology that will change lives. It will change the world. And it's our chance to put St Helens on the map."

Someone called, "This bloody meeting better not be about maps."

The crowd tinkled with laughter.

Mayor Brown gave a stiff nod and held up her hand. "I'm sure many of you have questions, but we have someone much better qualified than me to explain everything. And, I might add, he's a bit of a celebrity."

Bobby turned in his seat, searching the rows of faces, everyone else likewise was craning around to see, when one of the government suits came striding down the middle aisle. Bobby gasped. It couldn't be. His body tingled with excitement. When he'd spotted those suits talking to the mayor, he hadn't recognised him. This guy looked so different now – his hair and beard were neat and tidy, he was slimmer, healthier, he even looked hygienic. He'd had a total makeover. But marching towards the stage was the same startled scientist Bobby had printed on his t-shirt.

"He's spunky," Chook whispered.

"Everybody," the mayor said, "please give a warm welcome to Doctor Albert Manning. The man who made first contact with aliens and brought their technology to the world. And the man who is going to put St Helens on the map."

3

APPLAUSE AND MURMURS PEPPERED the room as Albert trudged up the stairs to the stage, tugging at his shirt collar. This suit was over the top. It itched and made him feel like an imposter.

He stepped to the lectern and hundreds of eyes scrutinised him. I can do this, he thought, looking around. Just breathe. Relax. People who are brilliant public speakers say this is better than sex. Obviously, they're idiots.

"Good evening. I'm Dr Albert Manning. Two years ago I decoded the first message from aliens and I revealed it to the world."

The crowd stared at him, blankly.

He was sweating uncontrollably and his pulse was racing, but he pushed up his glasses, took another sharp breath and tried to stand taller. Around the corners of the hall he checked for signs of the soldiers. Not even the faintest glimmer of them could be seen. He had told the major it was a terrible idea to bring them. If this went wrong, people might be hurt.

"I'm here to talk to you about a very exciting government initiative." He pointed at the word on the big screen behind him. "And I'd like to invite you to participate in this *opportunity* of a lifetime."

Grumbles washed over the room and people continued to glare.

He honestly envied them. Living in their perfectly isolated town that could be easily cut off from society meant they had won the lottery of science experiments. "If you choose to be part of this, it'll change the world."

He glanced down at the teenage kid squirming in the front row. The boy's crossed arms suddenly dropped to his sides and exposed a t-shirt with Albert's face on it. He sighed. There would always be haters.

———

After his *accident*, he'd found himself out of a job. Not because the feds had dragged him away, but because informing the world of Earth's greatest event was a fireable offence, according to HR. Apparently, it contravened work's social-media policy. Everything had to first be approved by Betty, head of digital.

As days turned into months, Albert rarely moved off his couch. Dirty teacups were piled over his coffee table. The government's decision to neither confirm nor deny his video's authenticity caused him overwhelming frustration. His phone became a mutant limb connected to his hand as he scrolled through comments about his broadcast. Quite a few seemed positive and he tried to cling to those. But many people felt entitled to assassinate his appearance; lots believed the video was a hoax; and some were just crazy, weaving Blixitor's message into a tapestry of their conspiracies. Drinking tea seemed to ease his anxiety – though he'd developed quite a dependency on English breakfast.

Three months after the broadcast, his phone vibrated in his hand. A private number appeared on the screen. "Hello?"

"Is that Doctor Albert Manning?"

"I'm not allowed to do media interviews," he said, leaning over the coffee table and checking his current teacup. A cold inch of tea lurked in the bottom, along with his last bag.

"Actually, we would very much like to interview you."

He took a cold sip. "How much are you offering?"

"Doctor Manning, I'm from DFAT. We'd like you to come into our office."

He winced before downing the rest of the tea. "I've already been interrogated. The government knows everything, even the colour of my underpants. And currently they're brown because I can't afford washing powder. So please, update the file."

Ending the call, he slumped into the couch, sighing. He should get himself together and go to the shops, but if another alien tour bus spotted him, he'd self-immolate. Those bastards were relentless.

His phone buzzed again and, swiping, he put it to his ear without speaking.

"Doctor Manning? Hello? Are you there? ...I can hear you breathing."

"Yes?"

"We'd like to offer you a job."

Albert squeezed his eyes shut. He shouldn't have mentioned his underpants. "Why would the Department of Foreign Affairs and Trade want to give me a job?"

"With the Department of Defence, we're establishing the Department of Alien Foreign Technology, otherwise known as DAFT. We need someone special and your name has come up."

When the military four-wheel drive dropped him inside a high-security compound, he was excited and frightened to be following two armed soldiers to an office where a woman in a pristine uniform greeted him with a firm handshake.

"I'm Major Wong," she said. Her dark eyes shone with fierce intelligence. "And I run a very tight ship, Manning. No leaks." She leaned close, gripping his hand tighter. "Why the powers above recruited you, is beyond me. I think they're fools. Your actions jeopardised our nation."

Shaking free of her hold, he forced a smile. He had hoped this might go better. Wasn't his public shaming enough? "Well, it's lovely to meet you too," he said. "But my name is *Doctor Manning*."

Her eyes flicked over his face, at his ironed shirt and best jeans for a good twenty seconds, an eternity, before she gestured to a chair. "Batter up."

Behind her desk, she explained the department had created this lab to decipher Blixitor's codes. "For months, only small pieces of the puzzle made sense, but slowly, our best minds translated that unfathomable number soup into something comprehensible." She pressed her lips together, in what Albert guessed was a smile. "Your alien's message is the blueprint for flying invisible cameras. The extraterrestrials want to spy on us."

Albert shifted uncomfortably in his seat, remembering his interrogation.

"Obviously, this is problematic." Tapping her fingernail loudly on the desk, her eyes gauged him. "Anyone who would allow an alien species unrestricted access to our planet is a total banana."

Albert nodded. That made sense from a military perspective, but science preferred to share knowledge.

"If," she continued, "we *were* to allow these aliens a tiny portion of restricted access, we'd never permit invisible cameras, especially ones which could fly." Her face was poker blank. "If you did, you are a banana."

Albert sighed, understanding the intent of her banana.

"However." She smiled again, tight-lipped. "Our government is extremely impressed by the aliens' blueprints. The codes have jettisoned other projects into the future. Our military camouflage is next level. The Australian government is—"

"Totally bananas over it?" he offered.

She stared daggers. "*Enthusiastic* about receiving more codes." Her voice was firm. "In national interest, we're enacting the alien's request. Within strict parameters."

Albert nodded, excited. What was his role in this? He wanted to ask, but felt like an amateur player in her strange game.

"The alien cameras are under our control with limited scope and range." She smiled, genuinely for the first time. "Those ETs have no idea, but the first sign this experiment turns crackers, I'm sending that tech to the cactus farm."

Albert nodded. "Understandably."

"I'm glad you agree" – she gave another tight smile – "because your job is to liaise with both the public and the aliens."

Albert's eyes went wide. "I'm going to talk to aliens?"

"Welcome aboard, *Doctor* Manning. And please don't fuck it up this time."

———

Albert stared out over the sea of faces. "Together we can change the world." He was getting into this. These people were listening. Some were smiling. "When I received the message from outer space..." The screen behind him flicked to a frozen image of Blixitor. The slimy green toad-like figure was smiling with sharp teeth. A gasp escaped from the audience.

"Those aliens better not wanna come here," someone called from the back.

"Don't worry," Albert smiled in a way he hoped was sincere. "It would take them over a thousand years to arrive."

The Aboriginal man sitting in the front row, shrugged. "My people have been here for over sixty thousand and it didn't stop you idiots turning up."

"I'm sorry about that." Albert pulled at his collar again. "The alien's message," he said to the crowd, "contained some amazing information. They sent us codes for totally new technology." The screen behind him changed to an image of scientists in lab coats standing around a prototype car. "Imagine going on a road trip without feeling any potholes." Albert smiled as the next picture appeared. The car floated in the air. Murmurs of approval washed through the crowd.

At the back of the hall, next to a large wooden box, stood the major. She nodded at him to continue.

"The aliens have requested to learn about our people." The TV screen changed to a shot of St Helens Bay with a family playing on the beach. The sand was white with calm water lapping the shore, picture-perfect. "They want to see you living your lives. You have the chance to show intelligent beings from another planet that we too are intelligent."

The crowd began to whisper, nervously looking around the room as though aliens might jump out.

"Aliens are not coming here." Albert held up his hands. "They want to study us from afar. They planned to secretly film you with cameras, but our government respects your privacy." He smiled at them. "You have rights. And one of them is the right to know you're being filmed. So to keep the aliens happy, you must pretend you don't know you're being filmed."

A buzz of confusion rippled through the audience.

"What?"

"That makes no sense."

Albert glanced at the balconies on the hall's sides, guessing the soldiers had been positioned there. "The aliens want to film you as though you're in your natural environment. Think of this as a documentary." He nodded at everyone. "When you watch David Attenborough, you want to see things as they are in reality, not chimpanzees hamming it. Looking at the cameras ruins the illusion. It's called breaking the fourth wall."

He watched the kid with the t-shirt in the front nervously lean over to whisper something in his friend's ear, and then glance around. Albert followed his line of sight to a particularly attractive lady standing behind the cake stall. How could he have missed her? She was stunning.

"Your town is lucky," he continued. "It's going to be the test site for some exciting new technology."

"Flying cars?" someone called. "Can I have a red one?"

"Unfortunately, the hover car is still in development."

The crowd grumbled.

"Good people of St Helens," he said. "I will now unveil something amazing. Something I hope impresses you." He nodded at the cake stall lady. "Alien technology."

The hall clicked into darkness, and several people oohed as kids giggled before a loud crack from the back silenced them. Major Wong had crowbarred off the lid of the wooden box and from its opening shone pink light, bathing the crowd in a soft glow.

People twisted in their seats. "What is that?" more than one asked.

A massive eyeball rose out of the box, the size of a beach ball, moist, fleshy and veined. Its glowing pink iris glared at the audience. People gasped and shifted uncomfortably in their seats. Albert knew the thing looked hideous; it was so organic it could've been plucked from a giant corpse. But he loved it, this marvel of technology. Children started to cry as the glistening and radiant sphere hovered over their heads, defying gravity. Fearful murmurs swept the room as the eye drifted above and slowly spun to reveal its rear side, gleaming almost translucent and filled with opaque jelly.

"Turn it off," a man screamed. "It's the devil!"

"There is no need to worry. It won't hurt you," Albert said in a gentle voice. He empathised with these people. Humans from the Middle Ages might've reacted similarly if they'd been exposed to today's computers and phones. "It's just a technologically advanced camera."

The TV behind him flicked to life, showing a direct video feed from the eye's pink iris. The audience saw themselves reflected on the screen. Some people relaxed, realising its function, but the babies continued to howl. The hall lights blinked on and the eye continued to hover in the air, watching.

"This is one of ten cameras that will be monitoring your town."

Chatter erupted through the room.

"I don't want that thing stalking me."

"It looks like a flying anus."

Give them a chance to process, Albert thought, watching a couple of ten-year-olds scramble under the eye, trying to wave into its iris while seeing themselves on the screen. A teenage girl with blue hair took out her phone and pouted a duck-face selfie in front of it. He nodded to himself. It'll be fine. They just need time to adapt.

The man in the front stood up. "My people have put up with a lot," he said to Albert. "But I wanna say this." He pointed up at the pink eye. "I don't want any arseholes from outer space watching me. I'm going fishing."

"Everybody, please." Albert held up his hands.

The eye above him turned in his direction, looking at him.

"If you don't want to take up this opportunity, you may have to leave St Helens."

More people started to stand to leave. "It's not an opportunity," someone called. "It's a bloody experiment."

"You will be paid for the inconvenience," he said.

They weren't listening.

He leaned close to the microphone and said loudly, "You will be paid a lot."

The crowd stopped, the noise died down at once.

"How much?" someone asked.

"Each taxpayer will receive $500,000."

Some faces glanced at each other, smiling. Two fishermen high-fived and some people began to sit. Others still seemed uncertain.

"Will kids get paid too?" asked the kid in the front row. "We've never paid tax."

"Um..." Albert said, scanning the room for his boss. Children weren't part of the equation. Major Wong was holding a finger to the tiny speaker in her ear, listening intently, a massive frown on her face. "Speak to me later, kid."

The crowd began talking again.

"Please," he said. He had to speak even louder into the microphone. "I want you to consider this. It's a lot of money for only six months of your life, just doing what you normally do. Nothing extra."

Albert noticed the attractive lady at the cake stall smiling delightfully at him.

"If you don't want to participate in this opportunity," he said, "the government will relocate you for six months, but without the bonus money. Information desks are around the hall if you have any questions. But you have two weeks to decide, before we begin broadcasting."

The mayor came onto the stage. "I'm sure you all found Doctor Manning's proposal very interesting." She smiled. "Thanks for coming, everyone."

As Albert stepped off the stage, no one clapped. He pulled at his collar and tie to loosen them. He really hoped his communication had been clear enough for everyone to understand.

The crowd stood and intense chatter filled the room. Groups were glancing in his direction, then up at the still hovering eye. Many people were heading to the info desks. Albert excused his way to the back of the room towards Major Wong, but also to the cake lady. After all this, he could murder a cup of tea.

"Excuse me, doctor." The Aboriginal man tapped him from behind. "I'm Bill."

As their hands shook in a firm grip, Albert said, "I understand your reservations with participating, but it will be a great—"

"I'll take your money," Bill said, cutting him off. "But a word of advice." The old man looked heavily into Albert's eyes. "Cut the bullshit. This is no opportunity for our town. It's yours and the government's." He nodded in the direction of Major Wong standing at the back of the room.

"But everyone will benefit from—"

"Save your speeches for the stage." Bill pointed at the floating eye. "I know you can't stop this from happening. It's bigger than you. But I'll tell you this: the moment you invite strangers into your home, you open yourself up to a whole lot of strange shit."

"It's really only a camera—"

"I'm going fishing." Bill walked off.

It's natural for people to be reluctant, Albert thought. He looked up at the eye still hovering above the room. This would change the entire world and, more importantly, it was going to change the way the world saw him.

He'd nearly made it to the cake stall when the kid in the t-shirt jumped in front of him with a ginger in tow.

"What's the deal with us kids not getting paid?" he demanded.

"We gotta live under 'em things too," said his friend, nodding at the hovering eye. "We deserve some cash."

Albert looked them over. "Sorry, what are your names?"

"Bobby."

"Chook."

Both kids stuck out their hands. Albert took the time to shake each one and said, "I'll tell you what, kids, I'll ask my boss now." He pointed at Major Wong.

"Do that," Bobby said. "Because we know something else is going down. And this shit is messed up."

"Thank you for your enlightening feedback." Albert smiled and walked way. Every town had its delinquents.

The woman at the cake stall was just finishing with a customer. As they walked away, Albert began to have doubts about approaching her. Would she be for the initiative? If she was against it, this could go terribly.

"Hi," she said. "Would you like to buy a cake to support St Helens High science classes?"

"Do you have any tea?"

"I wish." She laughed out a strange honk.

My god, Albert thought. She sounds like a goose.

"I could use a cup myself." She smiled. "But unfortunately no."

Albert surveyed the space-themed array: red Mars cakes, Saturn doughnuts with an orange ball in the middle of them, moon cakes with white puckered icing. "I'll take a Saturn."

As she passed him his change, she held his hand. "It's a pleasure to meet another physicist. My name is Grace."

"Albert." He shook her hand, thinking, is it possible she's beautiful and intelligent? "What are you currently working on?" he asked. It definitely wasn't his best line, so he regrouped. "I've read that just north of here, off the coast, physicists are using seismic vibrations to test ocean depth. Are you involved?"

"Well, I do like good vibes." The pink tip of her tongue poked through her perfect teeth as she smiled again. "But currently I'm working on something much more exciting. I'm the science teacher at our high school.

"Oh," he said, disappointed. "That's interesting."

"Today, my year seven class and I made these cakes."

Albert took a bite of his doughnut. It tasted dry and stale. He forced himself to chew and smile. "They're very nice."

As she leaned forward to rearrange the cakes, Albert copped an eyeful of cleavage.

"Actually," she said. "One of my senior classes might find it very informative if you came in to explain a few things. You know, because you've worked with radio telescopes."

"Of course," he said and swallowed the dry doughnut. "I mean, I would love to, but I'd need to work out a time. We're very focused on this trial."

She smiled. "The kids would really appreciate it."

Albert blushed and cursed himself for doing so. It had been a long time since he'd made small talk to chat up a woman. Come to think of it, he'd never made small talk to chat up anyone.

Major Wong suddenly appeared next to him. She nodded at Grace, before saying, "Doctor Manning, I need you on something."

"Excuse me, Grace." He stepped away.

The major said in a low voice, "I need you to clear the room." Her eyes glanced at the people around the hall. "Do it quickly."

"What? Why?"

She jutted her chin at the pink eye above them. It had floated after them from the cake stall, its pink pupil retracting as it focused in on them.

"It's begun broadcasting and we can't shut it down. The technicians think the Gatogrosians have taken control."

4

TWO WEEKS LATER

BOBBY WANDERED into physics class and took his usual seat next to Chook. "Did you see 'em this morning?" he whispered. "A pinkie followed me on my bike."

Chook smiled. "I bet you look delicious to aliens."

Over the last two weeks, ten of their classmates had disappeared to Launceston, but Bobby didn't mind, it meant Grace – or Ms Jacobs as he was meant to call her – would have more attention for him. She was writing calculus questions on the whiteboard and through the back of her white shirt he could see the colour of her bra. Maths is so sexy.

"Tucker." Dave poked him in the back.

"What?"

"Your mum's outside."

An eye the size of a beach ball, but slimy and meaty, hovered out the window two floors up, glistening and fleshy with veins like a huge human eye. Its pink iris contracted smaller to focus.

Dave laughed.

Bobby sighed and looked at Chook. "What's he on about? I can't see anything out there, can you?"

Chook glanced out the window. "Just the bay. Maybe Dave thinks your mum is as pretty as a picture."

Bobby smiled at Dave. "Are you in love with my mum? 'Cos I'm not gonna call you Daddy."

"Piss off, Tucker. I was talking about the pinkie."

"What pinkie?" Bobby put his hand on his forehead and made the shape of an L. "You're not meant to talk about them. Remember?"

"I'll fucking own you after class."

Bobby looked away. What a douche, he thought when a knock banged on the door.

"Everybody," Ms Jacobs said, "we have a very special guest today."

As she opened the door, the class groaned.

"Say hello to Dr Manning."

No one said anything. Bobby eyed over the doctor in his jeans, t-shit, his trimmed beard and stupid handsome face. God damn it, Bobby thought. Ms Jacobs was smiling at Albert in a way Bobby wished she would smile at him. Now his afternoon with her was ruined.

"Nice to meet you all," Albert said. "Ms Jacobs says you're learning physics. It's the absolute best to know how the universe works."

"You suck!" Dave called.

"That's enough," said Ms Jacobs. "Doctor, would you mind telling us all about the experiment starting today?"

He glanced at the pink eye outside the window. "Actually, I can't."

Ms Jacobs gave the class an apologetic shrug.

Albert cleared his throat, his eyes glancing around the room. "So kids." He smiled. "Are you ready to hear about the fourth law of thermodynamics?"

The class remained silent. Chook took out his phone and snapped a photo of the doctor and whispered, "Totally hot."

"Everything you love is going to die," Albert continued. "Your mum, your best friend, even your bike will rust and fall apart.

Chaos rules us all. Today, I would like to discuss entropy and when the universe ends."

"What about our pay?" Bobby called out.

"Excuse me?"

"For the experiment."

"Yes," said Chook "We're being experimented on too."

Albert looked at them both and Bobby saw recognition flash across his face before he looked back at Grace. She just shrugged again.

Dave stood from his seat. "You better pay us." He pointed at the eye outside. "Cos there's some weirdo from outer space watching us. It probably a paedo."

"David," Ms Jacobs said, tiredly. "Sit down. You're breaking the rules."

Bobby glanced at the eye, then back at Albert, who was frowning. Dave was completely messing up their chances.

"It is imperative" –Albert nodded towards the window– "that no one interacts with the eyes."

"But this isn't our experiment," Bobby said, "If we're not getting paid, we shouldn't have to obey your rules."

"This is an opportunity for everybody. Your reward will be showing an alien intelligence that humans also are a highly evolved and civilised people."

Bobby rolled his eyes at Chook and the whole class started to mutter.

"You're right," said Bobby above the chatter. "And I think the hope this is bringing to the human race is a massive responsibility. It shouldn't be taken lightly. We should do everything we can to make sure it goes right."

Albert nodded.

Bobby could see Kitty had turned in her seat and was watching him.

"We owe it to the world to do this," Bobby continued, "to do it right. And you owe it to us to do *us* right. You should pay us."

Ms Jacobs smiled at him. The entire class was beaming.

"C'mon, Doc. You know it's the right thing to do."

Albert rubbed a hand over his chin as he looked at Bobby, as though considering.

Bobby gave Albert another award-winning smile.

"Unfortunately," Albert said, softly, "the answer is still no. There won't be any payment made to kids."

———

Bobby sat on his bike next to Chook, squinting up at the moist, meaty pink eye floating over the playground as kids filed out of the gates. The aliens were probably making notes about him and Chook. Those freaks could stick it up their arse.

"Doctor Albert sucks," he said.

The hovering pink eye spun in their direction, its iris contracting.

"I think he's spunky." Chook shrugged. "I'm gonna totally add his photo to my collection of hot-dude pics. And that stuff about the death of the universe was interesting."

"Don't be a wanker. Look at that thing. The doctor's creepy meatballs are hanging right in our face."

Dave and Kitty stepped out of the main school building into the sunshine, holding hands. Kitty smiled at them and Dave glared with a sneer. Bobby thought, Dave, you wanted to own me. Own this. He began waving at Kitty again, smiling happily. He didn't care if last time had made him feel lame. Pissing off Dave was worth it.

"Another genius move from Bobby Tucker," Chook said, nodding at Bobby's waving hand. "Are you hoping he'll smash your face in?"

"He could try. But I'd have him."

"No doubt." Chook rolled his eyes. "C'mon, let's go see Baz."

As they rode away, the pink eye seemed to follow them, tracking their ride. Bobby glanced behind, seeing it. What the hell? He got off his bike. If he wasn't getting paid, the thing could punch it.

Suburban houses lined the gravel road. No gutters edged the street, grass melded into the blue metal. Bobby bent down and scraped up a handful of rocks.

"What're you doing?" Chook said, stopping next to him.

"Telling it to go away."

"You know, the universal language of love is throwing rocks at them."

Bobby threw, hard. Those aliens could die. The rocks flew high, scattering into a wide arc as they sailed directly for the eye. The eye zoomed up higher into the air as the rocks passed safely below.

"Piss off!" yelled Bobby.

It hovered, looking down, focusing.

"Stop following us!"

The eye started to back away, slowly.

"You know" – Chook smiled – "the doctor said we should pretend it's not here."

"The doctor is a waste of space." Bobby got back on his bike, their shadows stretched long from the sinking autumn sun as they watched the eye reversing slowly away.

"Okay." Chook sighed. "Can we go now?"

Baz's rusty caravan had been parked on his mum's front lawn for so long bushes and garden gnomes had sprouted around it like fungus. The boys dropped their bikes on the grass and Bobby banged his fist on the caravan's door.

"Baz. Open up." Bobby glanced around, checking the sky.

The screen door squealed ajar and a young man with a neat moustache and long sideburns peered through. "Well hello," he said, seeing Bobby and opening the door wider. Then he saw Chook standing behind him and his face darkened. "I suppose you both can come in."

The distinctively dank smell of Baz's business hit Bobby's nose as they stepped inside. A fan heater blasting away in the small room made it stuffier. They clambered around a small table on two bench seats. Bobby and Chook squeezed in together.

"I start a new job tomorrow," said Baz.

Bobby couldn't imagine anyone employing him. "Doing what?"

"Can't say. I'm sworn to secrecy." He smiled. "But it's in broadcast. Very glamorous."

"You're going to be on TV?" Bobby shook his head. As if. Nothing happened in St Helens "I call bullshit."

"Honestly, I can't tell you. It's hush-hush. Chook knows about keeping secrets, don't you?"

Chook crossed his arms and looked around the caravan walls.

Bobby glanced at Chook, who didn't look back, then at Baz, who acted like he'd said nothing. Weird? Did he miss something? "So, Baz, did you see those pink soldiers?"

"Bobby." Chook shook his head. "Don't."

He tried to read Chook's face, but it was blank, eyes straight ahead and avoiding his. "Never mind. Your pot was so good, I must've been tripping."

"Gentlemen, the new stuff I just got from my dealer, it's gonna blow your minds." Baz stood and opened a cupboard above their heads, pulling out a little bag of green buds. He opened it and a heady pungency slapped Bobby's nostrils.

"That's some serious dank."

"A sample before you buy?"

"Without a doubt."

Baz selected a chunky bud from the bag and Bobby slipped it into Chook's herbal vaporiser. The green light flicked on, and he started to drag. Instantly, Bobby's brain changed gears. Welcome to relax mode. He exhaled slowly. Outside, an engine revved as it pulled into the driveway. Kitty yelled something before a door slammed, and the car screeched away.

"And there she is." Baz looked at the ceiling. "My beautiful sister."

Bobby exhaled again, hoping she didn't come in. He had

enough dramas already. He handed the vaporiser to Chook, who shook his head.

"I've got a headache." Chook smiled, tight-lipped.

Bobby's eyebrows shot up. He had never seen Chook turn down free hooch. He handed it to Baz, who gave Chook a quick pointed look before his lips pouted under his moustache and he sucked back a lungful. The screen door squeaked open and Kitty stood there.

"The three amigos. What an unpleasant surprise." She'd said it to all of them, but her eyes were looking directly at Bobby, who swallowed. Then she turned to her brother. "I thought you stopped doing this" – she gestured at the little bag on the table – "now you've got a job."

"Haven't started though, have I?" Baz leaned back in his seat and smiled. Kitty crossed her arms, glaring at him.

Chook stood up. "Excuse me. I gotta visit the gents."

"Use the big gumtree away from the house," Kitty said, plonking herself next to Bobby. As her leg pressed against his, Bobby felt butterflies scrape in his gut.

Kitty said, "Mum doesn't like it when you blokes piss on her bush."

Bobby smirked. "I don't think Chook's into that."

Baz and Kitty laughed as the door swung shut.

Her hand brushed against his on the table. "I wanted to say how much everyone appreciates what you tried today." Her hand stayed next to his, connecting their hands so slightly they were only touching by a millimetre of skin.

Bobby felt as though electricity was pulsing through that spot. God he was so nervous. A couple of weeks ago, she didn't even want him here. "I was just doing what anyone would."

"No." She looked into his eyes. "You made us all aware of how unfair this is. Us not getting paid sucks, and I wanted to say thank you."

"No worries," he said, cursing his voice for squeaking. "Those bastards needed to know. Emperor Albert should pay us."

Baz got out of his seat and said, "I'll go see where Chook is at."

The screen door swung closed with a clunk. Kitty leaned into Bobby. Her lips pressed against his.

"Whoa." He pulled back. What the hell was wrong with her? "That's unexpected."

"Don't you like me?"

"Of course, but what about..." He looked to the side, stopping himself from saying more. Don't say *Dave*. Just don't. He's got the biggest fists in the world. Bobby glanced into Kitty's bright eyes. Her blue hair had fallen around her face and she wore a mischievous grin. "Why are you seeing that douchebag anyway?"

Kitty pulled away slightly, looking at the table. "I know Dave can be a jerk and a bully—"

"And a dumb arse freak."

She glanced to the side. "I was going to say, but he's strong. And" –She looked directly at him– "he's not into this." She pointed again at Baz's pot.

Bobby, very unsubtlety, slid it off the table and into his pocket. What was he doing? His questions were leading her further away from him. Be cool. This isn't amateur hour.

"And sometimes," Kitty said, "Dave can be very swee—"

"I was wrong. We don't need to talk about him." Bobby leaned in close again. "I'm far more interested in hearing about you."

Kitty smiled and put her arm around his shoulders, and their mouths met. He couldn't believe it, he thought, as her tongue darted against his. Only this morning, he was jerking off to the thought of Grace giving him maths tutoring. Now he could barely remember her.

Kitty moved closer against him, his hand reaching under her school jumper. He nuzzled her neck. She smelt so familiar, the scent of something earthy. In fact, she smelt a little like Dave.

"I've wanted to kiss you for ages." She put her mouth back on his.

Oh my god, Bobby thought. Before she came into the caravan she had probably kissed the big goon. Not only did she smell of him, his tongue would've been sloshing around inside her mouth. His saliva would still be oozing in there. It was like Dave was kissing him. Gross.

The door creaked open. Bobby pulled away to see Chook standing there with his arms crossed.

"Let's go," Chook said.

"Um... we're just doing some homework."

"Let's go."

"Relax Chook."

"Now."

———

On the dark horizon, the southern lights wavered like a curtain made of orange shimmering light. Bobby and Chook trod along a dark dirt path on the edge of the bay, phosphorescence glowing in the small waves and their phones lighting the track to the national park.

"What happened?" Bobby asked.

"Apparently, I'm acting like a child."

"Baz said that? He can talk. That new moustache is out of control," Bobby said, stopping. They sat on a rock overlooking the water and he pulled out the vape.

"He says I should try out a few men before I get into a relationship."

"Wanker."

"Sleeping with people everywhere isn't my thing. I want to take things slow. Really get to know someone. You get it, don't you?"

Somewhere in the bush behind them, a Tasmanian devil screeched a high-pitched wail into the night.

Bobby took a long drag, considering. It was so different from the way he thought of sex. All he wanted was lots of it. Now. Later. All the time. If he did it with his teacher - out of this world. With Kitty, also amazing. "Are you asking me for sex advice?"

"God! Really?" Chook glared at him. "You're doing the cool guy. Now?"

"Well, you know, I've totally got it." He grinned. "You saw how long it took me to hook up with Kitty. Thirty seconds."

"And if I hadn't interrupted, it would've been twenty seconds more before you splooched your undies."

"Next year is gonna be different," Bobby said. "We'll both be at Hobart Uni. I'll be shagging my way around the campus and I'm sure you'll meet some bloke of your dreams." Bobby suddenly realised that if Chook did, they would be spending time apart. "God, your man better like pot."

"I'm applying to Melbourne."

"What? Why?"

"'Cos I wanna meet people like me, Bobby. Hobart will be like St Helens, where it's just me, Baz and the bloke at the library."

"C'mon, Chook. It's Hobart. A massive city."

"Shhh." Chook held up his hand.

Footsteps were approaching. Bobby tucked the vaporiser and the weed into his undies. Then Bill stepped out of the darkness, carrying a bucket and fishing rod. "How's it going, boys?"

"All good, Bill. Any luck?"

"Nah, no bites. Reckon 'em pinkies have jinxed my catch."

The boys instinctively checked the skies to see if any were around, hovering.

Bill smiled at them. "So you boys chugging on the whacky, are you?"

"No," said Chook, too quickly. "We're just out on a walk."

"Don't drop a fat lie. I can smell it."

Another Tasmanian devil screeched in the bush.

"Alright," said Bobby. "It's true. We've had a few tokes. You gonna tell my mum?"

"Dr Cinnamon?" Bill laughed. "Not bloody likely. I wouldn't wanna cause her any alarm." He gave Bobby a quick wink. "So, have you seen 'em? The pinko troopers around town?"

"No." Bobby's eyes went wide. "There's more? We saw some at the meeting. They had machine guns."

Bill nodded, watching the horizon and the aurora flashing. Then his jaw hardened. Bobby followed his eye line. On the other side of the bay, he could see the distinct glow of a pinkie floating towards them over the water. Its soft glowing light reflected on the water, shimmering.

"All I know is this," Bill said. "When the authorities start lying, you should take matters into your own hands." He picked up his bucket and rod and started walking. "I don't wanna be 'ere when that thing shows up. You boys should nick off too."

As Bill walked away, Chook looked at Bobby. "No more rocks."

"We'll see." He took out his vaporiser, its light green and ready to go. He took a quick drag and handed it to Chook.

The glowing eyeball drifted over, illuminating Bobby and Chook in soft pink light. Trees rustled in the wind.

"Piss off," Bobby said to it, waving his hand as if he were shooing away a dog.

"I would like to ask you some questions," a robotic voice said from the eye.

Bobby stopped sucking on the pipe. Fear rose in his stomach. "What the f—"

"It's talking," said Chook.

"Your answers will help us in our research."

"We should go. Now." Chook stood up. "We're not meant to interact."

"I don't think so," Bobby said, dragging on the pipe again. He blew up a stream of vapour that clouded around the hovering fleshy eye. "We'll do a deal with you. We'll answer your questions if you answer ours."

The pinkie hung still for a moment. "How many questions do you have?"

"As many as I want. Now that was your first question. My turn."

"Don't do this," hissed Chook.

"Chill." Bobby smiled and turned to the eye, "First up, did you know everyone you're watching is getting paid?"

"Oh man." Chook blew vapour at the ground. "This is bad."

Bobby shrugged. "Fuck Doctor Albert and his rules."

The eye bobbed up and down a little, its iris contracting. The robotic voice said, "We understand. Thank you." The eye lowered itself closer to them. "Could you both provide your name and age?"

Bobby sucked on his pipe, then exhaled with confidence. "Bobby Tucker. I'm seventeen."

"Chook Adams." He sighed. "Seventeen as well."

"Alright." Bobby handed Chook the herbaliser and rubbed his hands together. This was going to be good. "Now we want proper answers," he said. "None of this we're-going-to-change-the-world crap. My next question is, do you wanna take over our planet?"

"No."

"You're lying."

"We have no intention to enslave your planet or species." The eye came closer to Bobby, just near his face, and the voice asked, "Will you and Dave have a physical confrontation soon?"

Bobby took a step backwards in surprise. "What the hell? Aren't you going to ask us questions about the planet?"

"Is that your next question?" the eye asked.

"Is that yours?"

"Your first answer is still required. Will you fight Dave?"

Bobby looked down at the water splashing on the rocks and shook his head, thinking for a moment. What the fuck did he and Dave have to do with this bloody experiment? "No, I'm not planning on it," he said. "But I will if have to. Why?"

"We are considering the outcome."

"Jesus. You're going to have a bet." Bobby looked at Chook, who shrugged. "What are my odds?"

"That is two questions. Our turn. Tell us, why do you find your teacher so attractive?"

Bobby took another involuntary step backwards. This was complete bullshit. How did they know? Anger started to bubble inside him. "C'mon Chook," he said. "Let's show these aliens some Tassie hospitality." He started unbuckling his jeans.

"Bobby, what're you doing?"

"They're invading our planet and our lives."

"So as a defence you're going to show them your cock?"

"No, I'm gonna show them the colour of our moon."

Chook grinned and followed his lead. Together they dropped their pants, turned and bent over to flash the eye the fullness of their arses.

Bobby yelled, "There's a brown eye for your pink one."

They reefed up their jeans and sprinted off, laughing into the darkness, leaving the pink eye hanging in the air.

5

SUN GLINTED off the station wagon as it puttered into the car park outside DAFT's headquarters and shuddered to a stop. Albert flung open the door and crossed over the bitumen, almost skipping. He'd had a fresh haircut and worn the suit. Today was going to be special. Everything they'd done for the last two years had been leading to this.

Yesterday, the experiment went live, and today, they were going to have two-way communication with Gatogrosians. The best part was that he was going to be the face of it. This would definitely get him closer to reviving his tarnished reputation.

He pushed up his glasses and glanced around for invisible soldiers as though he might glimpse one. He never did. Supposedly, they were standing guard outside the building. The clear-eye tech certainly worked, he thought. Either that or they were on a smoko.

"Hello?" he called.

"Morning, doctor," said a stern voice. "It's the big day."

"Yes, it is." He nodded, slowly, in what he thought was the right direction. Talking to invisible people was a whole new form of social awkwardness for him. The soldiers were probably making faces.

At the door, he swiped his access card and entered the main foyer. A new DAFT sign had recently been hung up behind the reception desk. He sighed. The last two weeks had been exhausting. After his town hall appearance, one of the eyes had gone rogue and started transmitting prematurely to the Gatogrosians. Major Wong had been furious. Her superiors had a lot riding on receiving more alien tech, but the town's population weren't ready to pretend they couldn't see the eyes. They needed time to process. So after Albert politely asked the crowd to leave and the hall cleared, she'd ordered, "End it, boys."

Sounds of soft piffs sprung from silencers on rifles. Punctures appeared in the eye's side like ruptures in a white bicycle tube filled with slime. It wavered in the air. Ooze dripped down its side and splattered onto the wooden floor. Then it fell, crashing into two rows of plastic chairs, scattering them. The thing bubbled and hissed in a pile of pink and white gloop.

The major barked into her headset, "Fix that bloody glitch."

Walking down the corridor in DAFT, he passed the boardroom where Major Wong and her chief project officer were sitting in front of a large screen watching footage from the previous night.

"Albert, get your arse in here."

He stopped mid step. Damn it, he thought, and turned slowly. What could possibly be wrong now?

Major Wong stared at him. "The bloody kids in this town think this is a joke."

"Why? What's happened?"

"First, there's this." Sally, the chief project officer, flipped around her laptop. She had collated hundreds of social-media selfies of teenagers posing in front of pink eyes. "Conspiracy theories are running hot over a secret alien invasion. Your job is to make sure everyone in this town is on board. They signed the NDAs. No one is to talk about this."

Albert glanced at the images. Some kids were pouting, some were pretending to hold up the eyes in the sky, and one kid had positioned the camera so when he bent his neck back, the pink eye was there instead of his head. Albert nodded. Some were pretty good. "Maybe," he began, "we set up an official-looking webpage and say that this is all for a movie promotion."

Sally looked at him with narrowed eyes. "Not bad, doctor."

Albert smiled with pride.

The major said, "Those pictures are the least of our worries. Do you recognise these idiots?" She pointed at the screen, paused on a close-up of two kids from the school. One of them was the boy who'd hassled him for money.

"Yes. They were in the class I visited."

Major Wong hit play. The screen showed the same boy talking with the eye.

"Everyone you're watching is getting paid," said the kid. The other one looked shocked.

Major Wong hit pause. "This is very serious, Albert."

He nodded, wondering how the hell he was responsible. He had done his job and told them explicitly not to interact with the eyes. The whole damn class had heard. "I wasn't even aware the eyes were equipped with a speech function."

The major glared at her chief project officer.

"Um... yes... well." Sally looked away and at the screen. "Neither were we at first. This organic technology still holds a lot of mysteries." She scrubbed through to the point where the eyes were speaking. The recording became garbled and glitchy. "And the Gatogrosians have been covering their tracks." The footage stopped on a close-up of the kids. Sally looked up at the major. "It is possible these two have been recruited into a clandestine group to undermine our operation."

The major looked at Sally. "You're suggesting they're terrorists."

She nodded. "We should pre-emptively strike against such possibilities."

Albert squeezed the bridge of his nose between his eyes. "They're just kids," he said. "They're not a threat."

"They're a pair of bloody bananas," Major Wong said.

Albert looked at her and nodded. He knew very well she didn't like bananas. "Yes. They are," he said, thinking that at least they were less threatening than terrorists. "And they couldn't organise a raffle. And they're also children."

She fast-forwarded the footage. "Look at this." It stopped on a frame of the two of them exposing their bare backsides.

"Um... that is a little in-your-face."

Major Wong's face was red. "It's outrageous! If the Gatogrosians have been offended, it may jeopardise our mission."

Sally said, "Shall I place two soldiers on them? They would never know. Until they misbehaved."

"These kids aren't a threat," Albert said. "They're kids. If we pay them," he said, slowly, "then they might take it more seriously."

"You've already proven you don't follow protocol." Sally's voice sounded harsh. "Major, I think we should take precautions and deploy the chaperones." Sally stood behind the major with her hands on her hips, trying to look important.

Major Wong glared at Albert. "I want you to sort this out, doctor. This is your job, not mine. Our first meeting with the aliens is this evening. It must go perfectly. Before that happens, I want you to warn these two delinquents."

"I'll have a chat with their teacher."

"Make sure they don't stuff it up. Because if this goes badly, it's your job on the line."

He looked at Major Wong. "They just want to be paid. I think if we can offer these kids something, it will pull them into line."

"I'm not paying yo-yos."

———

In his small office, Albert slumped into his chair behind the wooden desk. In his hands, he held a nice hot cup of tea. Sally was too trigger-happy to deploy soldiers. He took a sip, feeling the warmth travel into his stomach. This was just a storm in a teacup. They were kids, not some ridiculous fifth column. They hadn't ruined the experiment. He was still about to talk with aliens for the first time. Today should be celebrated, not turned into a witch-hunt.

He downed his tea before picking up the framed picture sitting on his desk. It held a selfie of him standing in front of the radio dish at Parkes. Look on the bright side, this is the perfect excuse to call Grace. He was pretty sure she was flirting after the lesson. Her hand had touched his arm when she said they should do it again. No one had touched him like that in years.

The clock in the corner of his laptop's screen read after midday; the school would be at lunch. He took out his mobile, fingers shaking as he scrolled to her number and pressed the screen.

"Hello? It's Albert."

"You've reached Grace Jacobs, please leave a message."

Beep.

Oh damn, he thought. But still, this was his chance to impress her with a witty message. Women loved funny men. He grabbed the first idea that came to him and began to sing. "Amazing Grace, how sweet the sound. To hear the voice that answered me." He stopped. What was he doing? He sounded terrible.

He ended the call.

"Fuck, fuck." He glared at the phone in his shaking hands. Not only was his reputation in jeopardy again, but he also looked like a complete knob.

His phone started vibrating with her name splashed across the screen. Surely, she couldn't have had time to listen to the message.

He lifted the phone to his ear. "Hello."

"Well, if it isn't the famous professor of the stars. Sorry I missed your call."

"Listen, just before, I kind of left a dumb silly message."

"Great. I'll have a listen."

"Sorry, but could you please delete it? It's really bad."

"Um... okay. I'll get rid of it." She laughed. "Right after I listen to it."

Albert forced himself to laugh and looked at the ceiling. "You know, you're really funny." He wanted to die. "I hope you like it." Don't dwell, he told himself. Move on. Major Wong would go ballistic if he didn't sort this out. "I need to ask you—"

"Would you like to come to my place for dinner?" she interrupted.

His eyebrows shot up and a smile beamed over his cheeks. "Yes. I would love to."

"Tomorrow at eight?"

Albert's hand was shaking as he wrote the details of her address. "Grace, I also wanted to talk to you about a breach. Two of your students have broken the rules." He went on to describe the two offenders.

"Is this *why* you called?"

"What? No. I mean, yes. No. But do you think you could speak to them? It's really important."

"I think it would be better if it came from you."

"But they respect you, you're their teacher."

"You'll have to speak with them yourself," she said firmly. "I'll inform Bobby and Chook that they need to visit your building after school."

She ended the call without saying goodbye and Albert stared at his phone, feeling uncertain if that had been a failure or a win. They were still on for dinner, weren't they?

———

Later in the afternoon, he came out of his office to see the boys sitting on couches in the main foyer. Albert thought they appeared very relaxed for a pair of delinquents who were supposed to be in trouble. They both had red eyes. After seeing them vaping pot in the footage, he knew they were stoned. He'd been to enough parties at university to know when someone had been smoking pot. And one of them was still wearing that goddamn t-shirt with his face on it. He already disliked these kids.

"Boys. Thank you for coming. Will you please come into my office?"

"Is this gonna take long?" asked the one in the shirt, stepping into his very small office. "Because I have homework. You know, our final exams are coming."

"When I go to uni, I want to become a professor like you," said the other. They plonked themselves down in the plastic chairs in front of his desk. "Your talk the other day nailed it for me."

"Thank you." Which one was Chook, and which one was Bobby? He wondered. And why did he agree to do this? He had no idea how to discipline kids. He could certainly go a cup of tea right now.

There was an abrupt knock tapped on the door. Major Wong poked her head through. Her eyes narrowed over the boys. "Albert, outside."

"Of course."

The boys raised their eyebrows and smirked as he stepped into the hallway. Major Wong closed the door behind him and Albert braced himself. Why couldn't she be one of those people who just repressed their anger until they had some sort of breakdown?

"Be hard on them, Albert."

"I will."

"But not too hard, you understand. They're kids."

"Firm, perhaps?"

Her eyes darted over him. "Well said."

She strutted away, and Albert sighed, opening the door. The t-shirt kid was leaning over his desk, holding the note on which he'd written Grace's address.

Anger jumped into his throat. "Put that down!"

The boy dropped it on the desk and scooted back to his seat. Albert eyed the kid and wanted to say more but stopped himself. He had to remain focused.

"Last night," he said, sitting down and breathing deep for a few seconds, "two adolescents broke the rules. They were seen exposing themselves to an alien eye."

"Exposing themselves?" T-shirt kid shook his head, confused.

The other followed his lead and also shook his head.

"Yes, Chook." Albert took a guess at his name. "It's very serious."

"He's Chook." Bobby pointed.

Chook asked, "Did someone send a dick pic to the aliens?"

"We can prove it wasn't us." Bobby stood up and started unbuckling his belt. "We'll show you ours so you can rule us out."

"Sit down. No one is showing anyone their privates. And no one has sent any penis photos to aliens," Albert said in a firm but calm voice. These two feckless idiots were going to cause him more trouble with Major Wong, he could already tell. "They very disrespectfully flashed their bottoms at the eye."

"I don't understand," Bobby said, wide-eyed and sincere.

"Me neither."

"You think we flashed our bums at an eye?"

"That's preposterous," said Chook. "I feel uncomfortable. I want you to call my gran."

Albert smiled. These little bastards were intentionally undermining everything he wanted to achieve but now he had them. "We have footage. Evidence."

Chook swallowed. "I don't want you to call my gran."

"Wait," said Bobby, rubbing his hands over his chin, as if weighing things up. "You have footage of our bums?"

"Of course we do. We collect all the footage that is recorded."

"You filmed our bums?" Bobby said again.

Albert straightened in his chair, trying to appear more authoritative, and took a deep breath. He knew where this was going. God, he wished he could have just paid these delinquents in the beginning. "Not intentionally," he said, "but this is a serious breach of our agreement."

Bobby leaned forward. "But you collect footage of kids showing their bums."

"It wasn't me. I didn't film it."

"You know what that sounds like, doctor."

"It's not like that." He glared from one to the other. "You were the ones who did it."

"Listen," Bobby said, "I don't care about your bloody experiment. You're not paying us, remember? I won't sit here and be blackmailed into silence by a group of government mega-paedos."

Anger rose in Albert's throat. "I'm not..." he began slowly, then stopped. "Just get out."

"Thanks, doctor." Bobby stood to leave. "Good chat."

Chook got up to follow him. "Don't tell my gran."

———

Albert stepped through the black doorway into the broadcast studio, fuming. Those little bastards were going to cause trouble. He entered the large room that had been rearranged to resemble the set of a TV news channel. Bright studio lights illuminated a very serious-looking desk. Behind the desk hung a massive photo of the Earth. The set designer had explained that the red-and-blue colour palette had been chosen for its calm but authoritative feel.

Albert had lifted his eyebrows, dubiously. "Is colour interpretation universal?"

Her eyes had narrowed. "What do you mean?"

"Well, these colours could represent aggression to an alien culture."

"Doctor, you do your job and I'll do mine," she'd retorted before strutting away.

"Albert! Hurry up," Major Wong shouted from the front of the room, hands on her hips.

To her side, an eye was strapped to a tripod so it couldn't float away. It was waiting for Albert to perform and transmit his communication. Wires connected the eye to a nearby screen.

"Did you warn those bloody yo-yos?" The major asked.

"Um..." He looked to the side and nodded. "I talked to

them." Not a complete lie, he thought, but how could he explain that they had just been accused of being mega-paedos? He wasn't going to touch that. The situation clearly required more thought. "You could say it went as well as you would expect."

"This had better be under control. No fuck-ups."

Albert nodded. "None whatsoever."

"Good." She walked away, listening to her earpiece. Albert considered how she might've reacted if he had told her the truth. He'd probably be out on his arse.

Sally stepped into the light. She wore a smug grin. "Here is your script."

"My script?"

"Yes," she said slowly, "for the words you're going to say."

"I know what a script is. I thought I'd wing it."

"Albert, this is tightly controlled propaganda. Think of it as news." She took his arm and led him towards the set at the front. "We don't want them to know what's actually going on."

"But it's meant to be a discussion between two alien life forms meeting for the first time. We need to exchange ideas. That's how conversations work."

"Albert, protocols must be followed. If you turn this into another incident, god help me I'll..."

"It was two years ago. I've learned."

"Stick to the script." She thrust the paper into his hands. "There will be a teleprompter on the screen next to the eye." She pointed to a big black monitor. "Read the words on the screen and you'll appear completely natural."

"Completely natural."

"Two minutes," someone called.

"No incidents." She turned and powered away, leaving him at the desk in front of the eye.

A young man with a neat moustache pranced towards him, holding a makeup bag. "Hi, I'm Baz," he said, powdering Albert's face. "Feeling nervous? I would be if was me talking to aliens."

"Um... no." Albert could smell something dank and musty on

him like the scent of his dad. He hadn't smelt it in years. "Do you have marijuana in your pocket?"

Baz stopped powdering and smiled. "Sorry, only enough for myself."

"One minute," someone yelled.

Baz whispered. "Come see me after the show. I'll sort you out." He spun on his heels and swaggered into the darkness before Albert could say that wasn't what he meant.

"Albert," Major Wong called. "No fuck-ups."

"Thirty seconds."

Albert swallowed and nodded, waiting for the black screen to come alive. Behind the lights he could see the shadows of people shuffling into position. This was it, he thought, sitting up straight. The moment everything had been leading to, the moment he'd hoped for when he received the first video from the Gatogrosians. This was the reason he had studied astrophysics. This was what people wondered when they looked at the stars.

The screen flickered to life showing two green-skinned humanoids, sitting on a plush couch. They were quietly chatting to each other, oblivious of Albert. To him, their heads seemed round yet slightly flat with a wide mouth and huge bulbous eyes on top, that sparkled with intelligence. One of them wore a glowing dress and sat with slender green legs crossed. The other wore a dark suit that sparkled like the night sky.

He pondered if they were the same species as Blixitor. These creatures appeared to be nothing at all like the previous Gatogrosian. That first alien had looked like a disgusting cane toad, while these seemed glamorous – frog like.

Words appeared on his screen. Albert took a deep breath. "Greetings Gatogrosians," he read, "I am Doctor Albert Manning."

The suited one quickly tapped the other on the knee, aware of Albert. "Hi," it said, "My name's Blax."

"And I'm Drixilio. Nice to meet you."

"We represent the Gatogrosian Council. How're things on Earth?"

Albert read, "We received your transmission from Blixitor and we would like to offer you our greatest..."

"Blixitor?" Drixilio asked. "Where's that?"

Albert stopped reading. "Um... he was..."

Blax whispered something to Drixilio.

"Oh yes, the famous xenopologist." Drixilio turned back to Albert. "He's dead, I'm afraid."

"Truly," Albert said, "I am deeply sorry for your loss."

"Don't trouble yourself." Blax grinned in what Albert assumed was meant as a wide reassuring smile, but was contradicted by his sharp pointy teeth. "It happened years ago. We've got a shrine somewhere on one of our moons, I think."

Albert nodded, hoping to appear understanding. He continued to read. "We would like to offer you our greatest gratitude for the information that you have passed on to us."

"Are you reading that?" Drixilio asked with narrowed eyes. "He looks like he's reading, doesn't he?"

Blax shrugged. "They all do it."

"Well, it's rude. You should talk to us."

Albert looked at them, then behind the lights at the dark silhouettes, searching for Sally or even Major Wong. He couldn't see any faces. This was exactly what he had feared. He looked back at the aliens. "Sorry about that," he said, ignoring the words on the screen. "What do you mean they all do it?"

"Who were you looking at?" Drixilio asked.

He remembered Sally's words about protocol. "No one."

"Yes, you were. We saw you. You specifically looked away to get someone's attention. Who was it? We want to see them. Hello?" she called. "Is someone else there?"

Albert swallowed, keeping his eyes on them. "I didn't—"

"Leave him alone," Blax said. "What is your question, Doctor-albert-manning?"

Drixilio interrupted again. "Doctor-albert-manning is a very long name." The slender alien leaned towards the camera. "Do you mind if we call you Bertie-man?"

"Um... okay," he said, puzzled. "Blax, what did you mean by 'they all do it'? Have you spoken with other alien species?"

They looked at each other and burst out laughing. Their sharp teeth sparkled in the light.

"Oh, Bertie-man," Blax said, "Hundreds. The universe is an enormous place."

Albert gasped, thinking about the brilliance of their statement. The universe teemed with intelligent life. "What are they like?"

"Oh, you know." Drixilio looked upwards. "Some of them are nice."

Blax grinned a mouthful of sharp teeth. "And some are nasty."

"Amazing." Albert shook his head at the implications. "Where are they?"

"Oh, we can't tell you. It would contravene our terms."

"But..." Albert stopped, gobsmacked. "You have treaties with all these aliens?"

"Not all." Blax frowned and looked at Drixilio. "How many?"

"No idea."

"But Bertie-man, we'd like to ask you something."

"Yes. Of course."

"How far are you willing to go with this..." He looked to the side as if remembering the words. "With this Grace-jacobs tomorrow night? Are you going to do it with her? We're very excited about it. We haven't seen your species perform any mating rituals yet. No one will leave their curtains open."

Albert looked at them, shocked. "How do you know about my date?"

"Our eye was watching her when you rang. We are very lucky to have captured it."

Albert felt a rush of blood come to his face. He wasn't supposed to be part of this experiment. He was a facilitator. It went against his scientific principles. "I don't want you to film me."

"Afraid it's not an option, Bertie-man. We need to document everything. And we're rather interested in seeing how you humans mate. To better understand your species, of course."

His brain rushed. He couldn't do this. He wasn't going to... How the hell would Grace feel about this?

"Now, Bertie-man. You would like some more of our technology, wouldn't you?"

"Um..." He looked around at the dark crowd of silhouettes watching him. This wasn't fair. He wasn't meant to be part of this. He was a scientist. "Not if I have to..."

"Cut, cut, cut," Major Wong yelled. "Disable the pinko."

A gunshot fired point blank into the eye. Goop exploded out the back of it. Slime splattered across Major Wong, her uniform covered in white-and-pink gunk. The screen with Blax and Drixilio flicked to black.

"Who the hell fired that shot?" Wong yelled.

"I did, sir," said a disembodied voice.

"Turn off your clear-eye."

A soldier, having hit the button to turn off his invisibility, sputtered into view like a hologram becoming solid. The man wore a black uniform and helmet that shimmered under the lights. In one hand, he held a pistol. With his other he saluted before adding in the softest of voices, "Sorry, sir."

"You're a bloody banana!" She strode off, covered in mess. "Albert," she yelled back. "My office. Now!"

Albert hurried past the soldier, who looked as if his mum had slapped him, and Sally filed in behind. The dead eye sagged, deflating and oozing gloop down the tripod and onto the floor.

6

IN THE SCHOOL HALLWAY, Bobby followed the line of students filing into the classroom. Stepping through the door, he noticed an eye hovering outside the window. Was it the same one that had talked to him? He couldn't tell. They all looked like fleshy, throbbing vein-filled balls of snot.

Ms Jacobs was thrusting a sheet of paper into the hands of each student as they entered the room. "Test day."

Chook groaned.

"Always a pleasure, Grace." Bobby smiled. She was looking as beautiful as ever.

"It's Ms Jacobs to you, Bobby."

"As you wish, Ms Grace Jacobs."

As they shuffled inside, Bobby directed Chook to two spots near the front, away from Dave who was at the back, taking up two desks with his tall body and massive limbs. Outside the window, the eye seemed to follow them.

"That's definitely the pinkie we mooned. I know it," Bobby said as they slumped into their seats.

"Uh-huh," Chook said with the enthusiasm of someone facing a firing squad. He was wincing at his paper. "This is gonna suck."

Bobby, still eyeing the pinkie, whispered, "It's definitely the one that wanted me to fight Dave."

"No one cares," Chook said, getting out a pen from his bag.

"You got another one?"

Chook shook his head, reading.

Kitty stepped into class. She's looking fresh, Bobby thought. Her blue hair seemed to glow. She lifted a paper out of Ms Jacobs' hand, grinned at Bobby and plonked herself into the seat on his other side. As she rummaged in her backpack, Bobby felt his stomach flutter. They hadn't spoken since the other night.

"How's it going?" he asked.

"Alright." She shrugged. "But, you know, I loathe tests."

"Kitty," Dave said from the back. "Come here."

"Nah," she said, without looking around. "I wanna be near the front so I don't miss anything." She winked at Bobby.

As Kitty turned her attention to her paper, Bobby felt hyper aware of her, the way her hair hung, her lips, and the pert shape of her body. He was sure Dave's eyes were burning a hole in his back. No way had she told Dave about their kiss, because if she had, Dave would've nailed that knowledge to his face.

Kitty crossed her long legs away from him, and while everyone looked at their physics equations, Bobby couldn't help looking at how her skirt had ridden a little higher against her chair. She's hot, he thought, staring. Very hot. This was the best show-n-tell ever. Was she doing it on purpose?

"Hey," he whispered. "Can I borrow a pen?"

"Sure." She handed him one without adjusting her position, her fingers sliding across his. Her touch was electric.

Bobby glanced down, trying to give her a subtle heads up about her skirt.

She saw his hint, glanced down, and then smiled without readjusting. "I'm hoping you'll give that pen back."

"I'd love to."

"Hey, Tucker," Dave called. "What are you saying?"

"David Brock," Ms Jacobs said with her hands on her hips.

"No talking during tests." She sat down behind her desk at the front of the class, directly in front of Bobby.

Kitty put her head down, concentrating.

Bobby heard Dave grunt and he, while trying to ignore Kitty's legs, began to calculate the speed of objects moving through space. But Kitty recrossed her legs, this time in his direction and he failed to even look at his paper. His brain flooded with images of where those legs might go before he forced himself to turn away. Grace was marking some other papers. From this angle, he could just glimpse down her shirt, catching some of her bra and cleavage. Oh my god, he was in love. It had finally happened. Was it possible to be in love with two women at once? The tent pole holding up his trousers said yes.

Jesus! Running out of time. He looked down and began reading. If a particle was moving along a line, what was its displacement in kilometres after x minutes? The answer? Definitely legs. Long sexy legs.

"Bobby?" Ms Jacobs placed a soft hand on his shoulder.

It sent shockwaves through his body. Excitement bubbled. Instinctively, he put his hand over his crotch.

"You seem distracted," she said. "Are you having trouble with this?"

"No." His words rushed out. "No problem at all."

"We can go through it together after class if you need to?"

Did she mean we, as in just the two of them? Alone? God! His hard-on ached.

"A couple of other kids also need some help." She took her hand off his shoulder.

"No, I'm fine," he said, realising he wasn't going to receive special one-on-one treatment for being an irresistible dunce. "I just need some more practice."

"Make sure you do that." She turned to the rest of the class. "Okay, pens down."

As students passed papers from hand to hand towards Ms Jacobs, Bobby buried his at the bottom of the pile. If a stack of tests moved to the front of the class at a speed of x, would the answers on paper b improve? He cursed Kitty and her long, so deliciously long legs. God. She still hadn't adjusted her skirt. His pants had become a peaked tent on his lap.

"Bobby, could you please stand up and tell the class what you learned from Doctor Manning?"

He coughed involuntarily. "Stand up?"

"Yes," Ms Jacobs said. "Tell us about the final entropy of the universe."

"Oh, of course," he said, starting to stand while awkwardly crossing his hands across his groin. "Yes. The slow death of everything."

Keeping his back to the class, he stood. Ms Jacob's eyes flicked down.

"The total entropy of the universe is ever increasing." He noticed Kitty also looking down, smirking. At least his boner wasn't increasing; it had already reached its peak and was now dying a slow death. The whole school would be laughing about this before lunch was over. Ms Jacobs also had a smile on her face, with her arms crossed. Oh god, this wasn't love. This was humiliation. He tried to hold Ms Jacob's eyes and ignore Kitty's as he listed theories about how the universe might end. And, he thought, the sooner it happened, the better.

———

"That class was diabolical," Bobby said to Chook, shaking his head. Kids were running across the playground, screaming. He just wanted to get on his bike and head home.

Chook grinned. "Your presentation seemed a bit stiff."

"Please shut up." Bobby ran his hands over his face. "If Dave finds out Kitty and I were flirting, I'm dead."

Chook laughed. "A slow universal death."

Bobby glared. "Just don't."

"It's cool. He was all the way up the back."

Then Bobby heard shouting.

"Tucker!" Dave came bounding out of the school's main entrance, towering over the other kids as they darted out of his way. "I warned you!"

Chook gave an apologetic shrug. "Maybe he did see."

Kitty came scurrying after him. "Dave. Don't."

Bobby watched the big boy striding towards him, the giant seemed to take metres with each step.

"We're gonna sort this. Now!"

Chook whispered to Bobby. "Wanna do a runner?"

Fear lurched in Bobby's stomach, but he tried to swallow it down and stand tall. "We can't outrun him. He's a total footy head." Besides, he was sick of people trying to tell him what to do. First the eyes. Then that weirdo, Doctor Albert. And now Dave.

The massive boy stood over him, like an adult, the way he always did. He totally uses his size to intimidate, Bobby thought. He was going to use it to his advantage. He'd call out Dave's bluff, or they'd end up in a blue, but either way, he was pretty sure Dave wouldn't wanna punch on in full view of the school's windows. His potential AFL career depended on good behaviour.

"Go on then," Bobby said, and put his chin up. "Punch me."

"I fucking will."

Other kids in the playground started to run over, chanting, "Fight, fight, fight."

This was exactly what Bobby wanted. Soon the teachers would come out. Hopefully, it'd be Grace.

A pink eye hovered low. Bobby saw it and knew this is what *they* wanted, those bastards.

Chook got in front of it, trying to block its view, saying, "What you see behind me is a fighting ritual occurring between two males of the human species, both trying to assert their dominance."

"Fight, fight, fight."

"Do it then." Bobby got right in Dave's face. The guy was going to back down, he knew it.

Chook narrated, "As you can see, each male is trying to claim ownership over the affections of the female." He nodded at Kitty, standing to one side with her arms crossed.

"Fuck off, Chook," she said.

The eye rose higher to get a clearer view.

"Is it true?" Dave asked Bobby.

"What?"

"You kissed her?"

So that was what all this was about, he thought. She had told him.

Kitty said, "Dave, I'm sorry."

"You don't own Kitty," Bobby said. "She can do what she likes."

"Tucker, you're out of line."

"Do it then, you snowflake fuckwit." He knew Dave would back down, just as surely as he knew Kitty didn't want to be with Dave. "She doesn't even like you."

Then Dave swung. His enormous fist collided with Bobby's mouth. A shockwave of pain ripped through his jaw.

"Fuck." Bobby spat red.

"Ladies and gentlemen," Chook said to the eye, "it's on like Donkey Kong."

Bobby swung back, his arm stretched out like a clothesline. Dave easily blocked it. Bobby swung again. Another easily blocked.

The eye hovered closer.

"Bobby Tucker's getting close and personal," Chook said. "Is this a comeback? Could he be triumphant?"

Then Dave jabbed. Bobby's head bounced backwards, then up and down as though Dave was punching a basketball. The hits kept coming, his fists whacking Bobby's face like a piston. Bobby couldn't think. His brains were being hammered. So he kicked out, booting Dave as hard as he could in the shins.

"Jesus!" Dave howled. "You kicked me. You're not supposed to do that."

Bobby tried it again, but this time his leg swung in a massive arc, sweeping his foot upwards as though he was trying to kick a rugby ball between the goalposts of Dave's legs. But the giant spun away, dancing aside in a move straight out of the AFL playbook and clobbered Bobby straight in the face with a haymaker. Bobby crumbled.

"Get up."

He couldn't. The grass was softer than a bed, and his face throbbed too much.

"Stay the hell away from of us." Dave began to walk off, reaching for Kitty's hand.

"Fuck off," she said, snatching back her hand.

"See." Bobby smiled with bloody teeth. He knew he would still win. "She wants to be with me."

"No, I fucking don't, you dickhead." She began to walk away with her arms crossed. "You can all just fuck right off."

Dave limped away in the opposite direction.

Bloody hell, thought Bobby, lying on his back while looking up at the eye hovering above. A failed test, an exposed boner, a lost fight, and being jilted by a girl he had not even gone out with. He'd read it wrong, all of it.

The kids who had been chanting dispersed, and Chook sat next to him on the grass. "In some ways," Chook said, "I guess I'm lucky there are no boys for me to fight over at school." He looked at the sky philosophically. "I think we need to vape."

"Baz's? No way" – he groaned – "Kitty might show up."

As he lay stretched out on the ground with his face throbbing, he saw the pinkie that had been watching drift away. Did any aliens actually bet on him? The odds of him winning were pretty slim. Then, through the window of his physics classroom on the third floor, he saw Grace. She was standing there and he was sure she had a smile on her face.

The setting sun glinted off the cars parked outside DAFT headquarters. Bobby and Chook sat on their bikes, leaning over the handlebars, watching the sky turn orange and pink. On their ride over they'd passed the vape back and forth, his lip had started to tighten and he could feel the meaty shiner forming around his left eye. But the sting of Kitty's rejection hurt more than the pain. Why did girls make things so complicated? Kitty liked him and clearly was over Dave – what was her problem? He had fought Dave and now he had nothing but this face full of pain and a weird feeling he'd done something wrong. If only he'd managed to kick Dave's in the nuts.

"I don't want to be here," Chook said, crossing his arms. "You sure you don't have any more pot?"

"We vaped it all."

They watched the transparent pink soldiers standing guard outside the building. Bobby thought they looked completely bored. He and Chook would probably be shot for entertainment.

"I don't really wanna see Baz," Chook said. "And Doctor Albert will probably come outside and hassle us."

Bobby shrugged. "Don't wanna be here either, but..." He glanced at the message on his phone. "This is where Baz said."

Chook's lips pouted like a cat's bum.

Bobby touched his puffy eye and flinched. It felt tacky. "Dave is going to cop it for this."

Chook rolled his eyes.

Bobby looked down at his trainers. Having Kitty as his girlfriend would've been amazing. At seventeen, he'd only ever kissed two other girls, both daughters of his mum's university friends who he'd see at barbecues. One girl had only done it because she was bored. "Better than listening to old doctors tell disgusting stories," she'd said before sticking her tongue down his throat. The other had sort of just happened while playing video games. And now Kitty. He didn't get girls, not yet, but he wanted to.

Baz stepped through the entrance and Chook sighed, looking away.

"Hello, gentlemen."

Bobby said, "I thought you said you'd got a job in TV."

Baz looked at his face. "What happened?" he asked, brushing his fingers over it with the lightest of touches.

Bobby pulled away, wincing. "Dave's fists."

"My little sister have anything to do with it?"

"Well, she didn't punch me." Bobby shrugged. Chatting about his relationship challenges wasn't high on his list of conversation topics. "Can we just buy some pot?"

"She can be annoying. Come inside. I have a first-aid kit."

They followed him across the car park with Chook lagging. Bobby did his best to pretend he couldn't see the soldiers. What the hell was Baz doing working for these guys?

They leaned their bikes against the wall near the door, stepped into the reception area where they'd met Albert, and followed Baz down a different corridor. Bobby really hoped the doctor didn't show up. After he'd called him a paedo, things might be a little awkward.

As they walked, Bobby noticed a door open as they passed. Inside, he glimpsed a pink transparent soldier and two other big blokes putting on what looked like black wetsuits. That must be where they get ready, he thought, where they keep their gear.

Baz opened a door ahead, and they followed him through. Bobby looked around the small room. There were lots of shelves containing pens, printer cartridges, paper and office supplies. To one side was a small desk with containers of makeup and a mirror on top.

"Welcome" – Baz waved his hands wide like a real estate agent – "to my studio."

"This is a stationery cupboard. You said you were working in TV."

"I am, but it's top secret. Can't say any more." Baz reached up to a shelf filled with boxes and pulled down a green first-aid kit. He unzipped it. "Now, while I fix you up, tell me what happened."

Bobby sighed and sat in a chair. As Baz began dabbing his face with cotton wool and red antiseptic, he explained how he'd stupidly goaded Dave into kicking his arse.

"So what's happening with you and my sis?"

"Nothing."

"Dave appears to think otherwise."

Baz touched Bobby's lip and he flinched. He didn't really want to talk about this. "Can we just buy some fucking pot?"

"You better have used protection. I don't want us to become related by accident. There, all done."

Bobby winced and stood up to check himself out in the mirror. He looked like a horror-movie victim, with red splotches all over his wounds. Baz tugged a small satchel of weed from his jeans. Chook slipped it into his pocket, handed Baz a twenty, and asked. "What kind of condoms do you recommend for Bobby? Ribbed for her pleasure? Extra thin for his? What does your sister like most?"

Baz smiled tightly, his little moustache stretching. "Have you tried one, Chook? Because from what I hear, you're a little frigid. I'd be willing to give you a little demo."

"C'mon, Bobby," Chook said. "We'll show ourselves out."

Bobby shrugged at Baz as they left. On the way out, Bobby stopped next to the room the soldiers were in earlier. The door was closed. "Hey, Chook. In 'ere."

"Let's just go," Chook said. "I wanna get high."

"C'mon. We'll just take a little peek. I saw some soldiers in here before, putting on weird wetsuits." Bobby cautiously pushed open the door and poked his head in. A pungent smell of body odour hit his nose but no translucent pink soldiers were in sight. Grey lockers lined the walls and a rack of black combat looking wetsuit hung from coat hangers in the middle of the room with a wooden change bench underneath.

"Hold your breath." Bobby stepped into the room and started flicking through the black outfits. Thin clear tubes ran all over the material.

Chook stepped in behind and closed the door. He looked around like a kitten entering a new room. "What the hell?"

"I know how to get revenge on Dave." Bobby pulled two suits off the rack and threw one at Chook. "Put it on. This is going to be next level."

"Bobby, is your brain broken? We are not doing this."

"Keep your voice down. It'll be fine." Bobby stepped into the legs of the suit he'd chosen and started zipping up the front. It was hard to get it over his clothes, but it fit snugly once he did. He pulled the hood over the back of his head. He felt like a scuba diver without an air tank.

Chook continued to glare at him, before sighing and starting to pull on his suit. "This is going to get us into so much trouble."

"How do we turn them on?" Bobby searched his outfit for a switch, patting himself all over. There had to be a button somewhere. Chook finished zipping up.

Voices came from out in the corridor.

"Bobby," Chook hissed. "They're going to come in."

Bobby slapped at his body in a panic, frantically searching for a switch.

The door handle started to turn.

"Fuck," hissed Chook, patting himself frantically all over.

On his chest, Bobby found a small round disc embedded under the material. It felt like a coin. He pushed it hard, just as two big men civilian clothing opened the door. Bobby's suit flashed for a second before disappearing. He looked down at his translucent pink chest and arms.

"Who the hell is that?" one of the soldiers yelled, pointing at Chook.

"Um..." He waved. "Hi."

Bobby slapped Chook hard in the chest and his body dematerialised into transparent pink. Bobby put his finger to his lips, signalling Chook to be quiet.

"Grab him," the other soldier said.

The two big men spread out either side of the room with their arms outstretched, snatching at the air, searching for the boys. Bobby and Chook quietly stepped up on the bench in the middle and tried to creep past.

Then Bobby had an idea. He swung out his leg in a full footy kick, like he had attempted on Dave, but this time unleashing the full brunt of force into the man's balls.

The big bloke crumpled.

The other came running over. Bobby leapt like a ballerina, swinging his foot in the most gracious arc and connected with the other man's crotch.

Out the open door, they sprinted through the corridor and slipped into the night. Back in the car park, they turned and watched the three pink guards at the building's entrance sprint back into the building as an alarm sounded.

Quickly, Bobby and Chook jumped onto their bikes and pedalled as hard as they could. Their bikes sped through the streets, appearing riderless, as though powered by ghosts. The alarm faded into the distance.

After they were out of the town, in the suburban streets, Bobby started laughing. "Fucking. Next. Level. Did you see how I booted those guys? Fuck, I wish I'd done that to Dave."

"They saw my face."

"Well, they can't now. Let's go visit Dave. I wanna get some payback."

Chook shook his head. "We are so busted."

"How can they catch us? We're invisible. As long as we stay stoned, we'll spot their pink soldiers from miles away."

They continued to ride through the streets. Bobby only had a vague idea of where Dave lived. He knew his house was near the footy oval next to the town hall, but he'd never been invited over. He was hoping to spot Dave's ute parked out the front. They passed a street sign, Gumtree Avenue, and Bobby pulled up.

"OMG. This is Grace's street."

"How do you know?"

"Saw it written on Emperor Albert's desk." Bobby smiled. It

hurt his lip, but he didn't care. "C'mon. This is gonna be awesome."

They coasted along further on their bikes until Bobby stopped outside number twelve. It was a single-storey house built of white bricks, with a garden out the front. Lights were on inside.

Bobby dropped his bike behind some bushes. "Let's take a peek."

"What? No. This is too much," said Chook.

"Shut up and keep your voice down."

Bobby ran up to the window and peered inside. Grace was still dressed in her jeans and shirt from school. She bent over to put something in the oven and Bobby took in the view. Fantastic, he thought. She couldn't see him, so he could watch as much as he wanted.

Chook's feet crunched over leaves as he walked up behind him.

"She's making dinner," Bobby whispered. "I think Emperor Albert is coming over tonight. Have a look."

Chook glared at him, whispering, "This is not my thing. I think we should go. You're being weird."

"She can't see us," Bobby said, peeping back through the window. Grace was standing in front of her open fridge. "Take a look."

"The things I do for you." Sighing, Chook stepped up beside him and glanced inside. "I am completely *not* okay with this."

Grace turned and glared directly at them.

"Shit." Chook ducked.

"It's okay," Bobby said in a low voice, keeping very still. "She can't see us."

Cautiously, Chook rose again and peeped through.

Grace came to the window, staring out. The boys held their breath. Her eyes scanned the street for a couple of seconds before she turned and left the room.

"She's going into the bedroom," Bobby said, and quickly

paced around the side of the house. This was it. He was going to see everything.

"Bobby," Chook hissed from behind. "What are you doing?"

"She's probably getting ready for her date. She might get naked."

"I know you think you're totally in love with her, but what about Kitty? And, bro, she's your teacher. And she's also a person. You shouldn't be spying."

"It's not spying, I'm appreciating."

"You're being creepy. I want to return these suits. Maybe we can convince them it was an accident."

They stopped outside her bedroom window.

Chook leant against the wall, staring at the night sky. "I'm not looking in. This goes against all the things I believe in."

"Whatever." Bobby peered inside. Grace stood in the middle of her bedroom, wearing only her bra and undies. Oh my god, this was it. "Come on," he whispered. "Take it off."

"You're such a weirdo. I wanna go."

Grace went to a dresser and stood in front of a mirror. Bobby realised in delight that he could now see all of her body. She picked up what looked like a remote control and pressed a button. Suddenly, her arms and legs warped, stretching longer, becoming skinnier, and changing colour.

"What the fuck?"

Grace's skin and hair turned green, and her eyes started to stretch apart, growing larger. Her mouth pulled wider and she smiled at herself in the mirror. Her teeth glistened, sharp and pointy.

"Oh my fucking god. Chook, you're not going to believe this."

"I told you – no."

"Chook, take a fucking look."

"No."

"Fucking. Do. It."

"This is not cool, dude. I know I'm not perfect, but I've got principles. I never spy on anyone and I only watch porn on weekends. I never let my gran clean my sheets and I've even stopped fantasising about the hot-dude pics on my phone. Everyone has got to have a line and this isn't right."

"Bloody hell, Chook. Look!"

Reluctantly, Chook turned and peeked. "Oh dear. That's not very good at all."

Bobby squeezed the bridge of his nose. "No. It's not."

"Your girlfriend is totally a space frog."

Bobby nodded, feeling a little sick. He watched Grace as she stretched out her green limbs, as though her muscles were sore. She wasn't really Grace anymore. Maybe she never had been. His skin felt slimy in the suit, as if his body was undergoing some elemental change. Jesus, maybe the aliens were gonna scoop out their brains or turn them all into frogs. He felt panicked. Maybe it had started already.

"Chook, we seriously gotta do something."

7

FLINGING the door to his station wagon closed, Albert hefted the roses he was holding, pushed up his glasses and took a deep breath. Grace's house looked nice, it was white brick, with a garden surrounding it. Just one date, he thought. All he had to do was act completely normal. Easy. Then, when she assumed he was a pleasant person, he could slowly reveal himself to be an anxious freak. And somehow convince her to have sex with him in front of aliens.

Walking up the garden path, he tried to ignore the pink eyes watching him. Two had followed his car and now another had turned up. He knew Major Wong would also be watching live as the footage streamed. Probably while munching popcorn, he thought. Just pretend no one is watching. That's all you have to do. While you seduce the most beautiful woman you've ever met. But pretending they weren't there was like talking to someone with a tattoo on their face. Sure, he could act like it was normal, but he'd still end up gawking.

He pressed the doorbell.

A text message buzzed in his pocket and he pulled out his phone. It was from the major. *Showtime.*

When Major Wong had summoned him into her office after

his chat with Blax and Drixilio, he knew he had messed up. As he walked into her office, she was standing behind her desk with her hands on her hips as if she were a gunslinger, paying no attention to the gunk splattered over her uniform.

Her voice had come out hard and even. "I want to be clear, Doctor Manning. This job requires serious meat and two very large potatoes." Then she dropped her voice. "I will not tolerate cupcakes."

Grace opened the door and smiled. "Hello, Professor of the Stars. Are those for me?"

"Of course." He handed her the roses.

She looked fantastic. Her hair was up in an elegant bun and she wore a rather revealing slinky black dress. Maybe this wouldn't be so hard, he thought. He had no idea what Grace was into. Maybe she'd like the idea of aliens watching. Hell, after he told her, she might even *want* to have sex with him. He could even say they were doing it for Earth.

Inside the house, the lights were dimmed. Tea-light candles had been placed on the coffee table and around the room. The place smelled of home cooking.

They sat on the couch. Outside the window, the soft pink glow of an eye stared at him. If only he could come up with a reason to close the curtains. Alright, he thought, let's get it out in the open. Then, maybe this debacle could be over and he could go back to his flat.

"Before we go on, I have something important to tell you."

"Ooh, great. This sounds like it's going to be one of these real conversations."

His phone beeped a text message. "Hang on." He pulled it out.

If you think telling her is a good idea, you're a bloody banana.

"Who is it?" Grace asked.

"Work." He flicked the phone to silent and slipped it into his pocket. "Nothing to worry about."

She smiled at him expectantly. "What is it you wanted to tell me?"

"Um..." He looked around the room for inspiration, then at the eye was outside. "Well, the experiment is going very well."

"That's what you wanted to tell me?" She raised an eyebrow.

His phone vibrated in his pocket again. Shit. "Hang on." He pulled it out.

Don't be a cupcake. Tell her you like her.

"Bloody hell."

"Let's put that away." She took it from his hands and tossed it onto the coffee table. "Now, Doctor, what did you want to say?"

"I wanted to... um..." He tried to think of some smooth words. Words that would make a woman quiver. He felt the eye hovering. Act natural. Act like they're not there. "Um, well. It's been a long time since I've met anyone like you."

"And?" She smiled.

"Well... actually, I've never met anyone quite like you. And what I'm trying to say is that I...well, I like you." There, he'd said it. Did he sound like an idiot?

"I like you too, Doctor."

Wow, he thought. She actually likes me. That's amazing. The last girl who had liked him had been years ago in uni.

His phone vibrated on the table, but he ignored it. He didn't know what to say next, but he knew he didn't want any more advice from Major Wong. Come on, genius. Think of something romantic to say. You've done a PhD. You can at least come up with some small talk.

A crash sounded in the other room, as if something heavy had fallen over.

Grace jumped to her feet with surprising speed. "What was that?"

"I'll go." Albert got up. Slowly, he walked in the direction sound had come from, towards a closed door. He gave it a shove and it swung open. Inside was a bedroom, tea-light candles flickered gentle light. Albert couldn't help smiling. It seemed Grace

84

was hoping things might go further too. "There's no one in here," he called. "And nothing has fallen over. But your window is open. Do you have a cat?"

Grace came up behind him and took hold of his hand. "No, I don't."

In the living room, he heard his phone vibrating. He could imagine the advice Major Wong was giving him. *Don't be a cupcake! Kiss her.*

"You seem popular," she said. "They won't leave you alone."

"Just work." He glanced at another eye floating outside the bedroom window. It was now or never, he thought. He could do this. Do it for Earth!

Albert leaned forward, readying his lips. Just as he came close, he thought he saw Grace wince. Did she? He pressed his lips against hers. It was like kissing a wooden plank. Then, when he pulled away, he saw her do it again. She completely winced, he thought. This isn't a good sign. No mating ritual talks about the opposite sex flinching.

"Did I do something wrong?" he asked.

"No." She smiled. "It's fine. I like it." This time, she leaned forward and kissed him. Her tongue darted into his mouth. Her hands squeezed his shoulders, feeling his arms. He felt her breasts press against his chest.

Then a beeper sounded in the kitchen; it was going off like a fire alarm.

"Shit," she said. "My roast. Wait here." She ran off to the other room, leaving Albert to look around the bedroom.

Well, that went well, he thought. He walked over to the dresser and looked at himself in the mirror. You can do this. Just ignore the eye floating at the window. You're not only doing this for Earth, you're doing it for yourself.

Grace stepped back into the doorway. This time, she was wearing only her underwear. She gave him a look that would've turned a cabbage into a heavy breather. Albert found himself acutely alert, with his heartbeat racing.

She said, "Doctor, dinner is served."

He stepped up to her, and this time when he kissed her, she didn't flinch. Their tongues danced while her hands tugged at his shirt. He pulled it off. She kissed his chest, her hands running over his body, exploring it. He struggled to lift her and she giggled as he carried her with awkward staggering steps to her bed. His hands explored her body. Caressing her with butter-soft hands, he gently tugged her closer.

As he reached down between her legs, he glanced out the window at the watching eye. Its iris widened.

————

Albert stretched out on the bed, ignoring the watchful eyes floating outside and looking at the ceiling instead. He was feeling extremely satisfied. Well done, Dr Manning, he thought. You are the pleasure machine. And those aliens, well, who the hell cares? Let them think what they want. His duty to planet Earth had been achieved with flying colours.

"Do you want to talk about it?" she asked.

"Yes! That was pretty damn good, wasn't it?"

In soft pink light, Grace looked puzzled. "Albert, I've had a lot of sex with many different partners. And I'm sorry to say, but that was pretty low grade."

"Low grade?" he repeated, shattered. He'd just performed for the universe. And what did she mean she'd had lots of partners? He'd only ever had four. How many had she had? And had she used protection with all of them? Was he inadvertently sleeping with hundreds of people in one giant orgy? With his previous partners his performance had been... well... they seemed satisfied. He wouldn't call himself a sexpert, but they hadn't called him shit.

"I want to give you some tips. You need to pay more attention to my needs. Like I did with you."

He folded his arms and considered jumping back into his jeans and his car and driving away. "I'm listening."

"The other thing I would say is you need to be intuitive. The female body requires a sensitive touch."

"Intuitive?" It was bad enough receiving feedback, but if she was going to go all hocus-pocus about vibes and energy, he was out of here.

"I think I might have something which will help."

Albert watched her naked butt as she slipped out of bed and sauntered over to her dresser. She glanced around for something. Her hand touched a spot and, for a moment, she seemed hesitant, as if she'd lost something.

"Did you move anything on my dresser?"

"Not at all. Why?"

She frowned and looked at the open window. "Never mind, I think I know where it is." She reached into a drawer and pulled out a slim silver cylinder.

Oh god, Albert thought. He knew what that was. He must've been terrible if she wanted help from that.

She climbed back into bed and snuggled close. "Have you ever used one of these before?"

"Um..." Albert looked at it. It was long and silver with a slightly bulbous head. It wasn't massive, but bigger than him. He shifted uncomfortably in the bed, thinking this was nothing to feel threatened about. It was just a toy. This was just part of the getting-to-know-you ritual. Then, in a voice which lacked any confidence, he said, "I'm open to new things."

"Good. This is going to be fun." She pressed the tip of it to her lips. The cylinder glowed.

Was she inhaling from it? He watched as she took a deep puff. His eyes went wide, realising it wasn't a vibrator at all, but a silver vape device with a helmet-shaped tip. He sighed, feeling completely relieved.

"Have you tried pot before?" She smiled, before passing it to him.

"Not since uni. It usually makes me sleepy."

"This won't, I promise."

The silver vape device in his hand looked completely alien and it had an inscription down the side in a language he'd never seen before. "How does it work?"

"You just put it to your lips and suck."

He glanced at the pink eye outside. Would Major Wong still be watching? Or would she have had the decency to tune out after he had started the first deed? If she saw him do this, it could jeopardise his position.

"Go on." Grace smiled. "This is going to be better than you can imagine."

Hesitantly, he looked down at the device. There was a small hole in the tip. He pressed it to his lips and the device began to glow before it shot vapour into his mouth as he inhaled. Instantly, he felt his mind begin to relax as if his brain were a series of tightly coiled knots that had begun to untangle.

"Wow." Then his thoughts started to speed up. This wasn't at all like the pot he'd smoked in uni. It felt different. Faster. Clearer. His mind was racing. "Grace, this is amazing."

"Good, huh?" She took it back from him and inhaled again.

In the pink light, his vision seemed a little fuzzy, but his mind was sharp. He was thinking about the universe and its vastness. He'd already heard there was proof of multiple civilisations and species. He wanted to meet them all. "Grace, where did you get this?"

"Back home."

"And where is that?" he asked, realising he knew nothing about her. Most of the time he had spent with her, he'd spoken about himself. "On the mainland? Melbourne?"

"Something like that." She smiled seductively. "Albert, I want you to put your hand down here." She took his hand and guided it. She felt warm and wet. "Now I want you to gently massage the top."

Suddenly his mind focused on the task. He was extremely

aware of his touch, as if his mind had synchronised with the nerves in his fingertips. Every sensation under them, her moistness, her softness, was acutely sharp in his mind. He heard her breath rising and falling, and he saw the glint in her eyes staring back at him.

"Good." She breathed out. "You're starting to get in tune." She leaned back and pushed herself into his hand. "Now I want you to play music with my body."

"But I'm not musical."

"Music is just maths, Albert. Maths and beauty." She thrust again. "Dance with me."

He could feel himself harden, but he was concentrating on the task because maths he understood all too well and he never wanted to appear low grade in her eyes again. Her scent was beautiful; he wanted to devour it. But if he could make this woman happy with maths, this was a challenge he was up for. As his fingers danced, he thought of the equations. One in particular came to mind, general relativity.

The pot was making his mind race. Everything else seemed to stop. Gently over her, his hand weaved in and out in the rhythm of gravity in space and time, sliding back and forth, breaking it down into small parts as though he was a conductor of an orchestra, his mouth pressed against her chest, sucking, his tongue flicking. His fingers played string-theory rhythms, and he felt as though her body had become one giant harmonic oscillator. Grace gasped. Albert was sure he could hear the fabric of space and time playing in a symphony. Then her body shuddered as if the universe was being torn apart and Albert felt so high because he was sure he saw her body flash green.

———

Albert rolled over in bed, waking. Without the eerie glow of the pink eyes outside, the room was dark. His head felt as if it'd been stuffed full of cottonwool. He wasn't going to smoke that again.

Admittedly, Grace's pot had led to the best sex he'd had – and arguably the universe had ever seen – but drugs messed with his head.

His mind was still racing. Leaning back on the pillow, memories of their encounter flooded his mind. She was amazing. He reached out for her, wanting to feel close and hear her breathing. His hand touched the empty bedclothes.

Under the closed door was a soft light. He could do with a glass of water; his mouth felt as dry as a sock. He got out of bed and stopped, hearing the soft murmur of voices. Who was that? Slowly, he pushed open the door and looked over the living room. His jaw dropped. How in hell? His legs began to tremble, his hands shook and his mind went dizzy. Was this even possible? He gripped the doorway because he might faint.

Sitting on the sofa with its back to him, sat a naked froglike creature with slender arms and legs. One of them is here, he thought. On Earth! It was illuminated by Grace's TV and seemed to be chatting with Blax and Drixilio, who were sitting on their plush couch, dressed in cocktail outfits.

I am too stoned, Albert thought, rubbing his eyes. This is not happening. I am never smoking that stuff again.

"So, sweetheart, tell us." Blax grinned on screen. "Is Bertieman fun to play with? I think he's delicious."

Drixilio cut him off with a wave of her hand. "What I wanna know is, did you really have the wonderful orgasmic experience we saw or did you fake it?"

"Well, a girl shouldn't say too much, but..." The slender alien leaned back against the couch and flicked her green hair. "With a little coaxing, the magic did indeed happen."

Albert's eyes went wide. Was that thing...? Was she...?

Another voice cut in. "Enough of this shit-talk." A fat Gatogrosian stuck his head in front of Blax and Drixilio, who shrugged at each other. The big frog licked its lips as its eyes flickered over the alien on the couch. "Fuck me, I've seen better acting from a sex robot. If your primate figures this out, it'll ruin everything."

"Sorry, Hextor."

"Does anybody suspect you? I don't want the council coming down on my arse."

"Two of my students. I saw them outside my window and they stole my bleeper."

Albert gripped the doorframe tighter. It *was* Grace. The world was spinning too fast.

"Sneaky little monkey fucks." Hextor smiled sharp teeth. "We'll be ready for them."

"Whoa!" said Albert feeling faint.

"Oh, now you're shitting me," Hextor said, looking directly at Albert swaying. "This is a complete cluster fuck."

Beneath Albert's feet, the floor swirled like an ocean before his legs buckled. Then the carpet collided with his face and blackness.

8

ON THE ROCKY point near the beach, Bobby blew out a cloud of vape towards the southern lights glowing green on the horizon. Ouch. His lip still hurt and things were seriously out of control. In one day, he'd been dumped and punched, become invisible, and seen his hot teacher going at it with Emperor Albert. Filthy gross. *And* she was a space frog. This would take years of therapy to get over.

Chook leaned over the edge of the rocks, watching the waves crash and the phosphorescence sparkle in the wash. He hadn't said a word since they'd legged it from Grace's place.

Bobby exhaled another lungful of pot and passed the vape back to Chook. A few more of these and it'd be like none of this ever happened.

"We're in so much trouble," Chook said, puffing quickly and looking about. "Those soldiers must be searching for us."

"Have you turned off your phone?"

"Yeah, but Gran wouldn't call now, she'd be asleep."

Bobby nodded, taking back the vape. His phone had two missed calls from his mum and four from Baz. If those arseholes at DAFT had questioned Baz, they'd probably know who they were by now. Chook was right. They were in a load of shit. But bigger things were at stake. Ms Jacobs was an alien, for fuck's sake.

He took another long drag. "I'm not ready to go home."

"We should take these suits back."

"Fuck no." Bobby shook his head. "We need to this figure out."

"Maybe we should tell Albert."

"The guy's an idiot. Besides, he would never believe us. You saw him, he's dating her."

"We could tell the soldiers."

"And what? They kill her? Or cut her up?" Bobby shook his head. She might be an alien, but that wasn't something he wanted. He still thought of her as a person, or a per-alien. "Plus, they won't believe us. We're just a couple of stoned high-school kids saying their teacher is an alien."

Back at Grace's house Bobby had clambered through the window and snatched the device off her dresser. Before she returned he'd managed to climb out, but he swore she'd looked directly at him through the window. And even though he knew she was an alien, she did look super-hot in underwear. Did that make him a xeno-sexual?

Bobby pulled out the device he'd stolen. It looked like a silver remote control with a few large buttons. Printed on its side was text in a language he had never seen before.

"How do you reckon it works?" Chook asked.

"Push the button, she changes." Bobby shrugged. "Push the other, she changes back. I'm guessing it's as easy as that." Bobby held it behind him in the direction of Grace's house and clicked a button.

Chook smiled. "If works from this distance, Albert is going to get the surprise of his life."

Bobby laughed. "Hell yeah. While they're going at it."

The wind started to pick up, blowing hard. Behind them, they heard a whirring noise like an electric engine humming.

They turned to see a glowing two-metre doorway suspended in the air and pulsating soft blue light.

"What the...?" Chook gulped.

Bobby jumped to his feet. "Next level."

"Don't go near it." Chook scrambled away.

The wind was getting stronger and being sucked into the doorway.

Bobby carefully moved closer. Leaves fluttered past him into the doorway, flashing white as they hit it. He could feel it pulling at him as if it were a magnet and he was metal. Up close, the glowing blue light swirled like oil on water. Inside seemed to be a deserted corridor with black windows lining the walls. He picked up a rock at his feet, hefted its weight and tossed it through. As it hit the glowing doorway, the rock flashed into solid light, and the door pulsed brighter. The rock landed and skidded along the corridor's floor.

"We should jump through," Bobby said.

"You've had a lot of bad ideas tonight. But this might be your worst."

"C'mon, Chook, it'll be awesome." The wind whipped around his face. "How many alien doorways have you ever gone through?"

The door suddenly disappeared. The glowing light vanished, the hum stopped and the wind died. The only sound was the waves splashing against the rocks.

"See," said Chook. "If we were halfway through, we might've been sliced in two."

"Must be on a timer," Bobby said, pushing the button once more. The door appeared again, this time to Bobby's right, in the direction he had held the remote. Bobby pulled out his phone and flicked on the stopwatch. His hands were trembling as he did. Nervous fear bubbled inside him mixed with excitement. Sure, this doorway could cook them like bacon, but it might take them to a place like no other. Nothing like this had ever happened in St Helens. Ever.

Chook folded his arms. "I'm not going in that thing."

"Don't worry, our teacher travels through it. It must be safe."

"She's a fucking alien, Bobby. And she's not our teacher. For all we know she might have eaten our real teacher."

The doorway disappeared. Bobby looked at the stopwatch. "One minute and twelve seconds. That's enough time for us to both jump through."

"I'm fucking not. No way are you getting me to do that. I've already done too many stupid things with you tonight."

"Chook. These things are invading." He looked at the silver remote in his hand. It felt cold and hard. "We've got to do something. We might be Earth's only chance."

"Fuck off. Tell the pink soldiers with guns. Let them deal with it. We're just kids."

"No, you're not. You're nearly eighteen. Time to step up."

Chook gave him a look that could've assassinated. "Like you did with Dave today? Look where that got us. We're running around like criminals."

"Ssshh." Bobby held up his hand. He thought he saw a light flash on the beach.

"It's fucking true," Chook said. "And you know it."

"Keep it down. I think someone is coming."

A torchlight came bobbing over the rocks as someone began to climb up towards them.

"Shit," hissed Chook, glancing at the rocks and shrubs. "Where should we hide?"

"Don't worry," Bobby whispered. "We're invisible, remember."

They sat very still as a large man came ambling up towards them. When he clambered up to the ledge where they were sitting, he stopped and dropped his bucket and rod. It was Old Bill.

Bill began to pat down his jacket pockets searching for something. Then, he slipped out a long joint and a lighter.

Bobby looked at Chook, who appeared as equally worried. They both knew what would happen when Bill sparked up.

Bill clicked the lighter and its flame licked the end of the joint like a fiery paintbrush. His eyes glinted at the hot ember as he sucked back a big puff and then blew out a cloud at the star-filled sky. Then he inhaled another.

Bobby held his breath. In a few seconds, Old Bill would be high and able to see them in their invisibility suits. And when he did, there would be loads of questions. He'd soon work out they'd stolen them. Bill knew Bobby's mum very well. They should do a runner, he thought, but how? There was no way they could escape quietly.

Fuck it. He stood up and said, "Ahh... G'day, Old Bill."

"Jesus!" Bill jumped. He turned, his eyes darting around, wide with shock. Then he focused on Bobby's pink see-through form. "Who the fuck are you?"

"It's me, Bobby Tucker." He put up a hand, to show he wasn't a threat. "Doctor Cinnamon's son. And here's Chook."

"Hi." Chook waved from his spot on the ground. "Nice to see you, Bill."

"Why the hell are you lads dressed like 'em bloody soldiers? I came here to get away from those idiots."

"So did we."

Bill took another drag on his joint and looked them both over. "You pinch them suits?"

Bobby nodded.

"What about your face? Them soldiers get you?"

"Nah." Bobby touched the tender spot near his eye. "I got into a blue at school."

"Looks like you lost."

Chook nodded. "He did."

"Shut up, Chook," Bobby said.

"What? It's true."

"I got him one good kick."

"In the shins."

"Boys." Bill held up a hand. "If you're dressed in them suits, I'm guessing you're in a shit-tonne of trouble."

Chook sighed. "Yes, we are, sir."

"But there's more to it than that," Bobby said. "We discovered our teacher is an alien. And this place is being invaded."

Bill's eyebrows shot up. "Bloody hell. History repeating."

Bobby explained how they'd stolen the suits and spied on Grace when she had revealed her true form. He left out the part about the remote.

"That's quite a story, boys." Old Bill shook his head, eyeing them both. "You've bitten off quite the mouthful. If things weren't so weird at the moment, I'd be hard pressed to swallow it." The waves crashed on the rocks as Bill took another drag of his joint. "My mob had a problem with invaders and it didn't end well. Lots of us died."

"What should we do?" Chook asked. "We're already in so much trouble. I think we should take these suits back and tell Doctor Albert."

"Don't normally give kids advice," Bill said, slowly. "The soldiers aren't going to be too happy with you nicking their suits. Not likely to believe your story about the teacher either."

Bobby said, "I reckon we fight the aliens. Blow up all the fucking eyes and stop the experiment. Then we figure out who the aliens are."

"Easy, tiger." Bill shook his head. "Violence only gets the people you know killed. And, besides, from the look of it, you don't seem too well equipped in the fighting areas."

Bobby grunted and looked at the ground. It was a decent point. "What do you suggest then?"

"Be smart. Gather your info. Document it. Then go to Albert. Now that fella won't have clue what to do, but his boss lady will."

"Are you gonna tell my gran?" Chook asked.

"Young fella, I'll leave that up to you. You boys are on a journey now. If you go home, the soldiers might catch you, but at some point, you're going to have to. But before you do, I'd suggest you find something which will prove your case." Old Bill bent down, stubbed out his joint on the rocks before he popped it back into his pocket and picked up his rod and bucket.

"Where are you going?" Chook asked.

"Not the end of the world yet, boys. There's fish to catch." He began to step over some rocks. "Good luck. And I never saw you."

They watched his torch flash over the ground and disappear around the headland.

"We're on a journey, Chook."

Chook sighed. "Whether I like it or not."

"Hell yeah!" Bobby slapped Chook on the shoulder. "This is gonna be next level. Get your phone ready, I want you to record this."

"I wanna call Gran first."

"Dude, she'll be asleep."

Chook shrugged as he pulled out his phone, switched it on and called. He waited for the message bank. "Hi, Gran," he said. "I know you might be worried. But I just want you to know I'm okay. I'm sorry I didn't call you earlier. I'm staying with Bobby tonight. I'll call you..." He paused, thinking. "I'll call you when I can."

Bobby tugged out his phone from his suit. His mum might be losing her mind with worry, but if she knew anything about what he'd done tonight, she'd be even more stressed. He wrote a quick text because if he called, she'd instantly pick up, and hit send.

Don't worry. I'm fine. Everything is going be alright.

This time he wasn't rebelling. He was saying no. No to the goddamn space frogs. No to their invasion. And no to being a good little boy. He was taking control.

He looked at Chook and smiled. "You sure you're up for this?"

Chook looked at him, unsmiling, "No, but whatever."

"We're gonna nail this bad boy."

"Hang on." Chook fiddled with his phone. "I'll stream it, so it makes a record online. That way if we die, people will know."

Bobby watched Chook log in to his account. The prospect of dying hadn't occurred to him. So far, this had just been mental and fun. But Chook was right. The stakes were big. If those space frogs were gonna invade, they wouldn't hesitate terminating him and Chook.

Chook held up his phone, flicked on the torch and pressed record. A red light blinked. Chook shook his head, staring at the screen. "I can't see you. You're invisible."

"Oh yeah." Bobby whacked the button on his chest. "Okay, people," he said into the camera. "Shit is about to get real." He held up the remote. "This device here opens a gateway to another world. We stole it off an alien, who's planning to invade our planet. So instead, we're gonna invade their planet. We're gonna prove this shit is happening and stop it."

Bobby started the stopwatch app on his phone and then, while holding out the remote, he said to Chook, "Ready?"

"Not really."

"Yes, we are." Bobby pushed the button. The doorway of blue light flickered alive before them. An electric hum filled the air. He grabbed Chook's wrist and grinned. "We're doing this."

Chook tried to smile, but had wide, worried eyes.

"On the count of three, we jump through," said Bobby.

The door hummed.

"One," they said together.

The waves crashed on the rocks.

"Two."

They took a deep breath.

"Three!"

Bobby and Chook sprinted towards the door. Chook held up his phone, recording as he ran. Bobby screamed with excitement, and together they leapt high. As their feet touched the glowing entrance, their bodies flashed. Bobby felt his body tingle all over while his limbs glowed white. Oh shit, he thought, as he felt light enter his brain. Had they just done the stupidest thing ever? In the next moment, he felt his body fall apart into billions of atoms before being dragged through the doorway like dust being sucked up by a vacuum cleaner.

9

ALBERT SAT in the meeting room with Major Wong and Sally wishing he were somewhere else. He didn't want to tell them what he'd seen last night. His hands shook as he poured a glass of water. If word got out Grace was from another planet, his reputation would be even more ruined – he'd be the idiot scientist who also betrayed the human race to space invaders. He sipped his water. A nice cup of tea would be better.

Words fired out of the major's mouth as if it were a machine gun, but his brain couldn't keep up. She was saying something about today's videoconference with the aliens and wanting more tech, he'd got that much, but the rest ricocheted away before he could catch it.

Last night had left his eyes feeling heavy in their sockets. He felt the opposite of happy and high; rather shit and sad. At least no one had mentioned the pot yet. God, that would make his standing in the scientific community even worse. Or would it? Carl Sagan had smoked it. Sigmund Freud used illicit substances. But then, so did zillions of drop kicks.

"Albert, I want you to get me something solid," the major said.

He nodded, vaguely understanding she was referring to tech.

"An advanced nugget – a prototype perhaps – that will make us Aussies world leaders. With this next exchange, I want us to become more than a superpower. I want us to become legendary."

"Uh huh," Albert murmured, jotting a note. "Super-legends." He glanced at Sally tapping happily on her laptop. This morning as his eyes had cracked open on Grace's pillows, disorientation flooded his brain. When he'd clocked Grace as an alien he had collapsed on the floor, but had woken in her bed, naked. "Hello?" he'd called, clutching the bedsheet close. Her clothes were scattered across the bedroom floor. On top of her dresser sat a dozen containers for makeup and face creams. "Grace?"

A magpie warbled outside. The house was quiet.

It is highly improbable she's not human, he thought. You can't believe it. After all, who wants to be known as the first man to have sex with an alien? But then, Grace did flash green. If he could just get access to last night's footage from the pink eyes, then he'd know.

"And this is all on you, doctor," said Major Wong. "You were meant to tell them to pull their heads in."

"I'm sorry?" He tried to replay what she'd been saying. "Could you repeat that?"

"Doctor Manning, I know you've been mixing work with pleasure, but do try to keep up. Those two adolescents, who you were supposed to pull into line, have pissed off with a pair of our clear-eye suits. Have you got any idea how to find two invisible delinquents?"

Albert shook his head. No, he did not. In fact, he wasn't sure what she was on about. He guessed now wasn't quite the right moment to ask about access to the footage.

"You're going to visit whatever freakish parents that spawned them" – she smiled tightly – "and explain their offspring are wanted as a matter of national security because they've stolen my military equipment."

Sally glanced up from her laptop screen. "We could lock them up as terrorists. This way we can bypass their guardians."

The major sighed. "Just find the idiots."

Albert closed his eyes and tried to think. Yes, Bobby and Chook were a pair of numbskulls. And, yes, their performance in his office still utterly annoyed him, but they were just kids. Their antics were nothing compared to aliens invading the planet. Grace might be one of millions living among them already. He really needed to see the footage. "Can't we just wait until their suits run out of power?"

"Doctor, try to not be such a slow-cooked noodle and wake up." Major Wong said. "Of course, we realise those suits will discharge soon, but when those kids do pop up" – she thumped the table – "I want their parents, teachers and everyone else giving them up."

Albert felt very tired. He glanced at Sally who avoided his eyes and looked back at her screen, typing. Had she watched him last night too?

The major said softly. "I understand you've had a tough night. We appreciate the efforts you've made for this project." She smiled, genuinely and Albert felt a flutter inside. She didn't smile like that very often. "You can rest assured we only monitored as much as we needed to. Once you initiated sexual congress, we left you to your devices." She shrugged with a small grin. "We figured you probably knew what to do."

Albert blew out a deep breath, relieved. At least they hadn't witnessed him getting high. "You see, I was wondering," he began. How was he going to word this? "Might it be possible to access the footage?"

The major raised her eyebrows. "Why?"

"Um..." Albert swallowed. He had to play this carefully. If he let on he'd seen Grace as an alien while being completely brain-addled and stoned, no one would believe him. And if they did believe him... Oh god. No one ever won an academic prize for shagging extraterrestrials. "Research purposes."

Wong smiled, quick and curt. "This is a workplace, doctor. How you spend your own time is none of my business, but there will be no access to DAFT's footage" – she paused – "for personal pleasure."

Sally shook her head, mouth agape and eyes wide.

Albert shifted uncomfortably in his seat. Comparatively, being suspected as a pervert was slightly better than the truth. But he still needed proof.

"Oh dear." Sally looked at her laptop. "Major, you're going to want to see this. Our idiots have uploaded a video."

They crowded around her laptop and she pressed play. On the screen, night footage streamed of waves crashing onto rocks as a voice said, off camera, *"I can't see you, you're invisible."* Then centre-frame, Bobby materialised into solid form wearing a clear-eye suit.

"Okay, people," he said. *"Shit is about to get real."* He held up a remote control. *"This device here opens a gateway to another world. We stole it off an alien..."*

"Goddamn these kids," said Major Wong over the video. "What are they playing at?"

"There's more," Sally said.

On the screen, a blue glowing doorway appeared. Albert leaned forward. What the hell? That had to be special effects because a stable Einstein-Rosen bridge was impossible. The shaky camera ran towards it and the boys jumped. The video flashed white and ended.

"What in god's..." The major said softly, still looking at the screen.

Was it possible they'd been at Grace's place? Albert wondered. There was that loud bang in her room, and then later, she'd asked if he had moved anything on her dresser. She seemed to have lost something. Could the boys have pinched that thing? And... what if they'd hung around? They might have seen them together. Albert swallowed, feeling uncomfortable.

"And, Major," Sally said in a solemn voice, "there are already over four million views."

"Cheeky little punks." Major Wong shook her head, grinning and leaning closer to the screen.

Albert got a sense she had just gained respect for the boys.

"Sally, inform our digital boffins this video needs to be added to our pink eye movie's promo material. We need to spread the bullshit thick and fast. The conspiracy nuts will have a field day if we don't."

In a soft voice, Albert asked, "Do you think they're dead?"

"Who knows? But finding them now is going to be impossible." She shook her head, still smiling. "Run the vid again."

They rewatched Bobby introduce himself and when he held up the device, the major said, "Pause. Zoom in. I want to see that."

"Looks like a TV remote," said Albert.

"Well done, genius. I can assure you it's not." She looked at him with level eyes. "Today when you're negotiating with the space frogs, you will get the codes for that."

———

Albert eased himself into the seat behind the studio desk. His brain no longer felt itchy, but he didn't feel ready for this. The major's plan bounced around his head. God, would it work? In front of him, a pink eye was strapped to a tripod like a hostage. Albert squinted into the harsh lights as he tried to make out the silhouettes of the crew. Okay, don't screw this up, he thought. Act like you know what you're doing. And don't let on that you know they're hiding something.

"One minute till transmission," someone called.

He wouldn't let those aliens get the better of him. He'd be strong, and definitely make no agreements to get down and dirty in front of them. He scanned the shadows. Where was that make-up kid?

Sally came striding out of the darkness. "Okay, we know the

space frogs are slippery bastards," she said, "so please stick to our plan and core messages."

Albert nodded. He didn't need to be told again. He had heard the details of Major Wong's plan as well. "Have you seen Baz?"

"We had to let him go. Don't worry, you look fine."

He attempted to pat down his hair. "Any chance you could help me get access to last night's footage?"

Sally's eyes narrowed. "Albert, I'm going to pretend you never asked me that."

Albert nodded. So his reputation now included being a dirty perve.

"Thirty seconds," someone called.

"Remember, if you must go off script, stick to protocol. Don't tell them anything. This is propaganda. We control the message." She stepped back into the darkness. "Good luck."

"We're going live in three, two, one."

The glamorous Drixilio and Blax flickered onto the screen. Blax's suit shimmered like the night. Drixilio sported a revealing glowing gown. Albert realised they appeared much like he had seen them last night on Grace's TV.

Blax leaned forward and grinned his pointy teeth. "Good evening, Bertie-man. Quite a performance last night. Can we expect an encore?"

"Um..." Albert could feel his face heating up. He didn't want to be drawn into this; he had to stick to the major's plan. "We have fulfilled your request."

"Oh, please say you'll see her again." Drixilio smiled. "Fun glowing toys, lots of play, it was quite special."

Albert heard the crew snigger. His face burned. Those aliens knew, as well as he did, that hadn't been a glowing *toy*. He glanced back and forth from the screen to the shadows behind where he thought the major might be.

"I think he's under control," said Drixilio. "Look at the way he's looking around. His masters won't allow him to seek love."

She lowered her voice. "We understand, Bertie-man. Just give us a signal."

Albert opened his eyes wide, puzzled. "I'm not under any control."

"Of course you're not." Drixilio winked. Then she whispered, "It's wise to play it safe."

Albert could see Major Wong shaking her head, so he read from the autocue to get back on track, "Greetings, Gatogrosians. Thank you for making contact with us again. We have fulfilled your request to present a mating ritual. We hope it satisfied your research."

"Why do they force him to read?" Drixilio rolled her eyes. "It's dull, dull, dull." She called out, "I want to speak to the wonderful Bertie-man we saw last night. Let him be free."

"Wait till he finishes," said Blax. "Then we'll get our turn."

They both smiled and nodded.

Albert continued. "Now that we have fulfilled your request, we have one of our own."

"Ooh." Drixilio clapped her hands. "I hope they want something unusual. Blax, what do you think it might be?"

Blax looked thoughtful. "Maybe to watch one of our mating rituals? Would you like that, Bertie-man? Do you want to see how *we* do it?"

Albert shook his head and took a nervous breath. He had to stick to the plan. This was it. Hit them with a request. He read, "We would like to access more of your information-coded technology. This time, for a light-speed engine."

Drixilio said, low, "Well, that's an anti-climax."

"Unlike last night." Blax sighed. "Primitives," he said and rolled his big frog eyes. "Always keen to get off their rock, but never to get their rocks off."

Drixilio laughed like a squawking cockatoo. "I guess they want to see other ponds. You know, the water is always clearer."

"Take it from me, Bertie-man, your home planet is your best

bet. There's only one that's perfect for you and that's the one you evolved on."

Albert asked, in his most polite voice, "Would it be possible to get the codes?"

"Unfortunately, no. A light-speed engine or ship isn't possible. We thought you primates had already worked that out."

Albert nodded in a way he hoped appeared to be thoughtful. They were buying it. They believed this was their request. "But previously you said your people met with other alien cultures."

"Oh, there're other ways, Bertie-man. In fact, some of us have already been to your planet."

Albert's eyes went wide. They were admitting it.

Drixilio laughed. "Look at his cute surprised face."

"You just never know, do you Bertie-man?"

They both flashed their sharp teeth.

Albert slowly shook his head. What did this mean? Were millions of aliens walking among them? "Do you have anyone here now?"

Blax laughed. "We're just messing with you. Why would we want to go to your planet?"

Albert felt his heart thudding with fear. "To invade and take our resources?"

"Possible, but no." Blax smiled. "Billions of uninhabited planets exist which are closer to us, full of resources and much bigger than your tiny rock."

Albert shook his head, he had run out of script. It was time to hit them. "Could you tell us how this works?"

Behind him on a screen, an image of Bobby's hand holding the remote control appeared.

"Oh dear," said Drixilio, softly. "The monkeys have a bleeper."

"Where did you get that?" Blax asked.

Albert smiled. "Perhaps you could tell us?"

Blax glanced nervously at Drixilio, who just shrugged.

Albert leaned forward. His eyes narrowed. "To continue this

experiment, we demand the codes for this..." – what did they call it? – "This... *bleeper*. Until we do the pink eyes will be inactive."

Blax shifted uncomfortably in his seat. "We'll have to get back to you, Bertie-man."

The screen flicked black.

Albert felt a surge of confidence. He had actually pushed them into a corner. This was fantastic. Then he did something completely uncharacteristic, he held up his fist at the black screen and raised his middle finger. The camera crew cheered.

———

The station wagon turned into the beach car park and spluttered to a stop. Albert flung the door shut and ambled over the sand towards the water. The soft rumble of waves filled the night air. He needed some space to think and this seemed as good a place as any.

The sand crunched under his shoes as he climbed over the dune. After today's videoconference, Wong had shut down the pinkies. She seemed a lot less happy about his success negotiating with the aliens than he'd expected. "They're playing with us," she'd said. "Their operatives are already here. I want the grunts searching for anything suspicious. If they see a space frog, they're to shoot it on sight."

All over St Helens, invisible soldiers in clear-eye suits were roaming the streets, but Albert knew, with the level of disguise Grace had employed, they had more of a chance of finding a talking wallaby.

After work, he had panicked and driven to Grace's house, in part out of fear for her safety, but also in the hope he might discover more information. When he arrived, no lights were on and as he stood at her dark window, peeking through, he could see all her stuff was still inside. The bedclothes were still strewn over her bed where he had left them and clean dishes were drying by the sink. The window had been left open with the trust of a country town, but he realised if she knew they were onto her, she might have already transported back to whatever planet she came from and taken any evidence with her. And if he was wrong, he'd just look like a creepy stalker breaking into her house. In fact, he already did by standing at her window.

Stumbling onto the hard sand of the shore, he stared out at the horizon where the stars met the sea. If he was wrong about Grace, and she wasn't an alien, accusing her of being so would ruin any chance with her – she would never forgive him. And if he was right, Wong would lock her up and he would never see her again.

Further up the beach, a fisherman was casting a line into the dark water. As Albert approached, he recognised him; it was Bill, the old man who'd spoken to him at the town hall that first night.

Bill gave him a smile. "Not many bites tonight," he said. "Hasn't been since 'em pinkies showed up."

Albert nodded. "Apologies. We'll have to look into how to make them less intrusive on the fauna."

"Not your fault, fella. This thing's much bigger than you."

"You know," Albert said, looking at the stars, "I was the one who discovered the aliens. Two years ago they contacted me."

Old Bill looked at him up and down. "You ever tried fishing?"

"Not since I was a kid."

Bill bent over, picked up another rod and handed it to Albert. The handle felt cool.

"Sometimes," Bill said, "it doesn't matter if you catch nothing. You just catch your thoughts." He pointed out at the waves. "Or your thoughts catch you. Go on, cast it."

Albert nodded, looking down at the rod. He flicked off the lock on the reel and cast out into the waves.

"Now just let it sit," Bill said, patting his pockets before he pulled out half a joint. "This stuff is deadly good. Wanna help me with it?"

Albert looked at the charred rollie between Bill's fingers. This would be the second time in two nights. He wasn't so sure. Or was this the gateway to being the next Carl Sagan?

"You'd be surprised at how it helps you see things differently." Bill sparked up without waiting for Albert's answer, took a long drag and blew out a cloud into the night. "Is a woman on your mind?"

"No. Not at all," Albert said, almost defensively.

"That's what brings most fellas down 'ere." Bill thrust the joint towards him.

Albert glanced around for pink eyes. Even though he knew they'd been grounded for the night, he also knew invisible soldiers were all over town.

Bill looked around too. "Don't worry. No one 'ere but us. I've got a way of knowing." Bill winked. "I won't tell if you don't."

Albert lifted the burning joint to his lips and inhaled. Holding the smoke down for a second burned. Then he began to cough. The mix of tobacco was rough on his lungs. After his coughing stopped, his head slowly began to relax. His mind uncoiled and he felt a completely different feeling from last night. It was slower and softer. After all the stress he'd been under, this was a nice reprieve.

"So who's the woman?" Bill asked.

"No one."

"C'mon, mate. Anyone can tell you've got a problem."

Albert considered Bill for a moment. Would telling him be such a bad idea? And yet... He handed back the joint. "Have you ever suspected someone isn't who they say they are?"

"You think she's acting a bit gammon, leading a double life?"

"Something like that."

"Well, personally, I'm a big fan of communication." He blew out another cloud and passed back the joint. "Maybe you should ask her. See how she takes it."

Albert took another puff before coughing again. His head was spinning. "Ask her," he said between coughs, then began to laugh at the idea of confronting Grace. What would he say? I know you're an alien. "If only you knew."

"What? That she's from another planet?"

Albert's eyes went wide. His throat felt suddenly tight.

"I think we've had enough." Bill smiled and lifted the joint from Albert's fingers, took one last drag, and stubbed it in the sand. He slipped it back into his pocket. "Am I right?"

"How did you know?"

"I ran into a couple of lads earlier, who had seen an alien."

"Bobby and Chook?"

"I can't rightly say, but 'em kids were shaken up."

Albert thought of the video he had seen of the boys jumping into the glowing blue doorway. If they had told Bill they had seen Grace as an alien, that proved it. "You have to come with me. We'll tell my boss."

"Tell her yourself. I ain't saying a thing to the government." Bill looked over the horizon and started winding in his reel. "Never did anything good for me or my mob."

"I understand, Bill, but this is bigger than us. It could affect the entire planet."

"Because your woman's an alien?" Bill laughed. "Fella, I don't know her, but one person rarely changes the world. If them aliens wanted to invade, they would've done it already."

Albert's head was spinning. Maybe he'd had too much.

Bill pulled his line in, slipped a worm over the hook and cast it out again over the waves. "If you ask me, your woman is scheming something else. Invaders don't make nature documentaries. They come, set up camp and take over. With lots of killing."

As Albert wound his own reel in, he reflected on Bill's words. Blax had said it wasn't feasible to take over their planet.

"Whatever the girl is cooking up, it's strange and bigger than you." Bill looked at him with soft gentle eyes. "Let your boss lady know. She's the smart egg in your bunch."

Albert felt a hollow pit form inside his stomach. Bill was right. He pulled out his phone and scrolled for the major's number.

10

AFTER WHAT FELT like milliseconds and also an eternity, Bobby stumbled out of the glowing doorway into a white corridor. He swayed, feeling blinded, but managed to keep his footing. Chook then lurched through behind him and slammed into his back, sending him flying. Bobby put out his hands to stop the floor from flying towards him, and the remote slipped from his grip and skittled down the corridor, as he landed with a grunt. Behind them the glowing doorway vanished.

Lying there with his cheek pressed against the cool floor, his whole body tingled. Only moments before he had been standing on the rocky point of St Helens Bay with the wind in his hair and waves crashing below him. Then he'd jumped through the alien doorway and felt every atom in his body being ripped apart, vaporised and restitched.

His gut gurgled. "Oh dear." He rolled over, breathing deep to stop his stomach heaving, and looked up at the ceiling, glowing soft white and glistening. "Worst travel experience ever."

Chook plonked next to him, cross-legged, clutching his belly. "Oh my god, your face."

"What?" Bobby touched his nose. "Is something missing?"

"No, but your bruises are gone."

Carefully, Bobby prodded around his eye where Dave had punched him. It was true. The pain had gone. His lip too. Bloody hell, he thought. That might have been worth it. He climbed to his feet. The walls were white yet slightly wet, leaving a little slime under his fingers. He looked closer. Tiny veins were throbbing inside the wall – green, red and blue with a jelly goo that seemed to be holding it together. Bobby poked and it wobbled like flesh.

"This is definitely not St Helens," Chook said, still sitting and looking about.

Bobby eyed the fleshy walls, "I hope we're not inside some creature's butthole." He ambled down the corridor to retrieve the remote. No, no, no, he thought, as he picked it up. Don't be. A massive crack had split the side. He slumped back next to Chook and showed him. "We have a little problem."

"What! Click it. Quick."

Bobby pressed the button. Nothing happened. No hum. No doorway.

"Oh man!" Chook said. "This isn't good."

Bobby looked at the broken remote in his hands then at Chook chewing his lip, staring straight ahead. If they were gonna get through this, they had to be on their game. They couldn't wig out. He put his arm over Chook's shoulder. "We'll work it out."

"What am I gonna tell my gran?"

He shrugged. "Sorry for being be late."

"I hate you."

Chook checked his phone for a signal, while Bobby went to explore further down the corridor towards the black windows. Up close, they looked more like holes in a tree, where the wall had grown around to leave a space and instead of glass it had a translucent membrane, shiny like a thin snot. It felt hard under his finger, yet wet and cold. Outside, stars shone clearer and more vivid than he'd ever seen. Turn it up, he thought. This is insane. Pink and blue sections clustered the sky. Then, he looked down.

"Whoa. Chook, check this out!"

An olive-green world swirled beneath. It looked like a space photo he'd seen online, the land and oceans blending together murkily. Excitement bubbled inside him. This is unbelievable, he thought, pressing his hand against the window, staring at the globe's slow spin. Floating around the planet were hundreds of huge long ships that looked like giant white sausages, longer than ten footy stadiums. This is next level. The furthest he'd ever been from home was to Melbourne for the weekend with his mum. Now he was in space. "Get ready, we need to document this."

"Fine." Chook sighed, climbed to his feet and held up his phone.

Bobby waited while he focused.

"Yo! Alien infiltrator, Bobby Tucker here." He swung his arms around like a hip-hop star. "We just landed on this alien space station. Now we're gonna show those freaky space frogs who rules the universe." Bobby paused and looked directly into the lens. "If you're wondering who: Bobby and Chook."

Chook rolled his eyes, watching the screen. "Bit cringe. Wanna do that again?"

"Shut up. Just flip it for a selfie."

As Chook did Bobby saw that behind him a tall frog and two smaller frogs were marching down the corridor towards them.

"Hello," Chook said, nodding at the camera. "We're probably gonna die."

"Hit stop," Bobby said.

"No."

"Stop."

"But I wanna say more. Like we're gonna totally be stuck here forever. And the froggy bastards are gonna eat us."

The tall frog hurried past, dragging the two smaller frogs by their hands down the corridor. It glanced over its shoulder with worried eyes before disappearing out of sight.

"Awkies," said Chook, as he slipped the phone back into his pocket.

"They're definitely gonna tell someone about us," Bobby said. "We should go invisible from here." He hit the button on his chest. It clicked, but nothing happened. He hit it again. Nothing. Hit. Still nothing. Oh shit. An anxious tension started to slide into his chest with a terrible ache. He looked over at Chook slapping his own chest.

Bobby smiled. "We may have another problem."

"I hate you even more."

As they crept down the slick corridor, the walls pulsed and Bobby tried his hardest to listen for footsteps and ignore his doubts building. Behind him, he knew Chook was pouting because of all his sighing noises. If anyone could be blamed for breaking the remote, it was Chook. He'd knocked him over. And, come on, this is an adventure. Stop acting like a sulky dog. Bobby took a deep breath. If you want anything in this life, you had to grab opportunity's balls. They'd done that getting here. Now they had to push on, document this bad boy and get home. Easy.

As the hallway curved, one wall had a large artwork on it that looked as if it had been tattooed into its fleshy surface. A green fist surrounded by a red circle with bold symbols under it: triangles, squares and weird squiggles. It all looked very angry.

Bobby pulled out the remote and compared the style of writing. "Check this out. Totally the same."

Chook looked at him with one eyebrow cocked and a face of complete disinterest. "If we die, I'm gonna say, 'I told you so.'"

Bobby walked on with Chook huffing behind him and stopped at a large horizontal crease in the slick wall. Above it a glowing sign stuck out displaying more geometric text. Beside the crease glowed a button.

"Get your phone ready. We're going in."

"Going in where? You don't know what that is..." Chook pointed at a window. "It might open into space."

"C'mon, Chook. Live a little."

"I want to live a lot."

Bobby grinned, holding his hand over the button.

"Just don't."

He slapped it. The crease stretched apart, opening like a

massive mouth. Tendrils of slime dangled around the door's lips, which lead into darkness. "See. We're still breathing," he said and stepped through. A musty smell hit him as his eyes adjusted to the dim light. The air felt warm and wet. Empty chairs and tables filled the room. Along one wall stretched a long bar and behind it, mounted on a wall were shelves containing bottles of every colour, some glowing. This place looks amazing, he thought. The only other bar he'd been in before was the Bay Hotel in St Helens, where his mum always bought him the same lame ginger beer. God, he hoped no one asked his age.

A wrinkly frog-man behind the bar croaked at them, loudly.

"Hello," Bobby said, slowly, trying to make each syllable clear. "I am from Earth."

The old frog-man croaked again.

"Me Bobby," he said, placing a hand on his chest. "Earth." He pointed to the stars outside the window.

Chook came in behind, recording on his phone and staring around like a wide-eyed kitten. The frog-barman gestured with a long green hand for them to come nearer. He placed two glasses on the bar, grabbed a large medicinal-looking bottle from the shelf and filled the glasses with a thick gloop then thrust the drinks towards the boys. The brown slop in the glass wobbled.

"You first," Bobby whispered.

"Are you fucking high? This whole mess is because of you."

The barman croaked something, grinned his pointy teeth and pushed the drinks closer.

"Yeah, but," Bobby said, "I came through the door first. You should drink it."

"I'm not touching that."

"Fine." Bobby nodded at the smiling frog-man, picked up the glass and sniffed. His face screwed up. God, it smelt worse than a rotting wombat. Just sniffing it was turning his guts inside out and would stain his nostrils for a week.

The frog-barman gestured to drink.

"Go on," said Chook with a serene smile. "What's the worst that could happen?"

Bobby winced as he put the cup to his lips. The smell was rancid, and as he sucked it back the warm gloop slid down his throat like thick mucus and sat in his belly like a lump.

Frog-barman nodded to swallow more.

"C'mon," Chook said. "What's taking you so long?"

"This is feral." Bobby was sweating. Quickly, he lifted the glass and swallowed the rest in one gulp. He looked up at the dark ceiling, eyes watering, trying to hold it down. Its warmth spread inside his gut. It felt as if he'd swallowed someone else's vomit.

The barman croaked at him.

Bobby gripped the bar tight while still looking up, and said loudly, "I don't understand."

The barman laughed in a deep croaking noise. "Give it a moment."

Bobby's eyes grew wide as he looked around the room, his mind spinning as he realised what he'd just understood. "Next level!" he said, as the sickness eased. He grabbed Chook's shoulder. "You gotta drink this. It's amazing."

"Are you insane? It smells disgusting."

The barman smiled. "Let him figure it out. So, tell me. Which system are you from?"

"System? We're from Tasmania."

"What the hell?" said Chook, looking back and forth between Bobby and the barman. "You speak frog?"

The old green barman sneered. "Your friend better watch his mouth. I am no more a frog than you a monkey."

Bobby whispered to Chook, "Don't mention the 'F' word."

"Don't say fuck?"

"No, you idiot. Don't say..." Bobby acted like a frog hopping. "Ribbit, ribbit."

The barman frowned. "Behave yourselves." He walked off.

"What's up with that guy?"

Bobby sighed. "Just drink your drink."

Chook made a face and eyed his glass of gloop.

A couple of frog-people in sparkling suits entered the bar and sat at a table. The barman went over to serve them and pointed at Bobby and Chook. The two customers looked over and burst into laughter.

Bobby waved and smiled. Through the corner of his mouth, he said to Chook, "Hurry up. Drink your feral mucus."

"I won't," said Chook, taking a sniff and making a disgusted face.

"If you drink it you can understand them. They already understand us. If you wanna get home, we're gonna have to talk to these people."

Chook took the most delicate of sips. His face screwed up. "No. I'm sorry. I can't."

"Down it. Now."

Chook glared at him. "Because you asked so nicely."

As Chook forced down lots of tiny sips, the bar started to fill up. Most of the patrons were frogs, but a few seemed to be from other planets. One looked like a massive koala creature that roared with laughter when it heard the boys were from Earth. Another was like a massive upright grasshopper and made clicking noises with its beak while it laughed.

A frog dressed in a sparkling suit sauntered up to their table. "Hello, boys. Allow me to get you a real drink." He clicked his fingers and said to the barman, "Glicks for the Earthlings."

Bobby stuck out his hand. "Bobby."

The frog-man looked at his hand and said, "My name is Gaxa." Then he also stuck out his hand, mimicking Bobby's outstretched one. Bobby grabbed his green hand and shook with a firm grip.

Gaxa's eyes went wide and snatched back his hand, rubbing it. "Earth-boy, this is how we do it." Gaxa held up his hand, as if for a high five. "You do the same."

Bobby got himself ready for a slap but Gaxa gently pressed his palm into his.

"It is a pleasure to greet you."

The barman placed three large glasses of glowing blue liquid in front of them. "Now, our glick." Gaxa smiled, holding up his drink. "A toast to the greatness of where we come from."

"Tasmania?"

Gaxa laughed. "Yes. Let's drink to Tasmania."

Bobby lifted his glass and sniffed. It smelt good, without even a hint of rotting puke. More like raspberries. He tasted it and the flavour tickled his tongue, sweet and delicious.

More aliens came over. Everyone wanted to meet them and try their handshaking. More glicks arrived.

"Oh, it's so rough," one said, laughing, shaking her froggy hand.

Bobby felt his mind speeding up, his pulse racing faster and his body relaxing. Chook had finished his gloop and they were telling stories about Earth. Laughter filled the room. More drinks flowed and as Bobby became lightheaded, he felt himself losing his ability to sit still, hopping up and down. Chook was taking it slower, trying to film some of the event with his phone, but Bobby kept interrupting him to take selfies, posing for several with the laughing koala and insect creature.

Later, as Bobby was dancing around pretending to be a monkey to massive cheers from the crowd, a frog-man barged in and glared at Bobby and Chook with angry narrow eyes. He looked a lot less glamorous than the others, wearing black trousers and a t-shirt that had that image of a green fist surrounded by a red circle. The angry frog slapped his hand hard on a table causing the drinks and empty glasses to rattle. Chook stepped backwards, holding up his phone.

Angry-frog yelled at the crowd, "End this cruel entertainment. Free the Earthlings! They don't deserve this."

Bobby swayed, the glicks were giving him confidence. He turned to Chook and nodded. "I got this."

"Sure you do." Chook rolled his eyes.

"I'm berry sorry," Bobby said, hearing his voice slur while his mind raced. He could do this. Be diplomatic. "You seem to have the wrong idea. These people are lovely."

The frog-man stared down at him.

Bobby didn't want to be 'that guy' but he had to admit that while drinking he might have accidentally broken about a million cultural taboos. "I didn't mean to offend."

"You offend your people."

This wasn't going well. He glanced at Chook who just shrugged, still filming.

"I'm Bobby," he said, swaying slightly and held up his hand the way the other frog-man had shown him.

Angry-frog ignored his gesture and yelled again at the crowd with a raised fist, "Free the Earthlings! End the cruelty."

"Mister." Bobby pointed, not quite straight. "I don't know even what you're on about."

"This is a publicity stunt." The frog-man gestured to the crowd and then pointed at him. "For the show your people are being exploited in."

Bobby squinted at him. "Do you mean the documentary?"

"Is that what they told you?" Frog-man scoffed. "Their show is the biggest across the six civilised galaxies. Everyone is watching you."

11

ALBERT BRUSHED his fingers through his hair, attempting to force it into a presentable state and took a deep breath. He would've preferred to be sipping a nice cup of tea, but this had to be done. Through the office door's window, he glimpsed the major hunched over her desk, bashing away on the keyboard and glaring at her screen.

Last night he'd sat on the sand, listening to the surf, waiting for Bill's joint to wear off so he could drive home, and considered exactly what he was going to say and do. He was going to knock, enter, and present the facts like a regular scientist. Nothing to it.

Raising his hand at a glacial speed, he gave delivered three sharp taps on the door.

"Yes!"

Opening the door a fraction, he poked his head through the gap. "Major, I would like to discuss something."

She frowned. "Our videoconference is in thirty minutes. We can do it afterwards."

"This might make a difference to the outcome," he said, stepping in and easing into a chair.

She looked at the ceiling and sighed. Albert had the feeling he was visiting the school principal's office.

"If this is about a pay rise," she said, "now is not the time."

"No, Major, it's something much bigger. Much more serious." He gripped his hands in his lap to prevent them shaking. "The other night," he began, "when I visited Grace Jacobs, she seemed somewhat odd."

"Doctor, I'm not one to offer relationship advice, but you're very odd yourself."

"Major, I have reason to believe she is an alien."

Her eyebrows shot up. "You think your girlfriend is a space frog?"

"She's not my girlfriend."

"Why?"

"Well, we're still getting to know each other, and—"

"No, you banana. Why do you think she's a space frog?" Major Wong leaned forward, her eyes darting over him as he explained that when he'd been having sex with Grace, she had flashed green.

"So what happened?"

"What do you mean, what happened?"

"After she revealed herself as an alien?"

"Then..." He took a deep breath. "I fell asleep."

Major Wong raised an eyebrow.

"I know it sounds incongruous that I would fall asleep after seeing an alien, but it had been a very exhausting night. I wasn't one hundred per cent sure I was seeing things correctly. It happened very quickly."

"Go on, go on," she said impatiently.

"Well, later I awoke to hear talking and peeked into the living room. There, I witnessed her in her true alien form. No flashes or anything. She was talking to Blax and Drixilio on the television."

"And then?"

Albert looked at his hands in his lap. "I fainted."

The major leaned back in her chair, looking at him for some time. Finally, she said, "These are serious allegations. Do you have any actual evidence?"

"Not exactly."

She looked to the side, clearly weighing up the situation. Albert felt butterflies in his stomach.

"And you only had wine to drink?"

"Well, I might have smoked a little something."

She crossed her arms. "Doctor, you have me very concerned. Our videoconference is in twenty minutes. I need you at the top of your game."

His eyes went wide. "It wasn't much." That was the truth.

Major Wong sighed again. "I shouldn't say this and I'm going to go off the record here, you understand? I'm going to tell you something about myself. I used to be an addict. Not drugs – gambling. But one addict knows another. And you have all the signs."

Albert felt his stomach drop. His mind was racing. He'd only had two puffs! The time before that was in first year at university at some house party where he'd spent the evening lying on a couch feeling even more socially inept. "But I'm not..."

"Doctor, you can't bullshit a bullshitter." She leaned forward. "I'm sure the schoolteacher *is* a little odd. She'd have to be if she likes you. But perhaps..." She looked at him with concerned eyes. "This has been a very stressful time. I'm going to recommend you speak with a psychologist."

———

"Ten seconds until we go live."

Behind the studio desk, under warm lights, Albert forced his best smile for the pink eye. He was going to maintain a cool confidence just like last time.

"We're live in three, two, one."

The screen flickered and there were Blax and Drixilio smirking on their couch, glamorous as ever.

"Greetings, Gatogrosians," he read from an autocue. "Thank

you for making the time. I hope you've had an opportunity to consider our request."

"Ooh." Drixilio clasped her hands. "He's all business today, isn't he?"

"Well done, Bertie-man." Blax grinned sharp teeth.

Albert's jaw clenched. The name-calling was starting to grate.

"It seems," Blax continued, "you set up quite a game for us to play. We didn't think you had it in you."

In the darkness of the studio, Albert knew the major was watching, waiting for him to land her the deal. "We cannot go any further with the experiment without you fulfilling our request."

"Now, Bertie-man, before we get to that, we want to ask, are humans ready for the universe?"

"I believe we are."

"But are you and your people really ready for what comes with being able to travel between planets? Because we think otherwise."

The screen cut to a video of a room filled with frog-people. In the centre was Bobby Tucker, dancing around the tables like a monkey.

In the studio, there was a collective sharp intake of breath. The screen cut back to the two glamorous smiling aliens.

Blax said, "Now, is that a sophisticated human who has evolved enough to accept the responsibilities that come with an interstellar cultural exchange?"

"I, um..." Albert began. Those little bastards were ruining everything.

The screen cut to another image of Bobby, huddled in a corner, heaving vomit onto the floor.

Blax smiled. "Despite how this may appear, we have not done this to him. He did it to himself."

Albert said, "I humbly apologise for any offence caused."

"Oh, Bertie-man, you're going to have to do better than that. You're going to have to really convince us that you're ready."

Albert looked at the smiling aliens and thought quickly. "We

humans have been studying the cosmos for eons. We, as a species
are—"

"Blah, blah, blah," said Drixilio, waving her hand. "Try
harder, Bertie-man."

He thought about all the great breakthroughs in science, the
philosophical minds who had changed society, and the brilliant
artists who had given insight into the human psyche and said,
"There's no doubt that most of us are idiots."

Blax nodded. "Agreed."

"But some humans are intelligent, diligent and respectful.
Some create work that has transformed our world. Unfortunately,
the rest of us just want to party. But it's the good times that keep
us going and bring us together."

"And which are you, Bertie-man? Intelligent or
nincompoop?"

"I would like to consider myself to be part of the solution."
He could feel the eyes of the whole studio on him. He knew the
major would be thinking about his earlier admission. "But I have
to confess, I do like to have a good time too."

Blax and Drixilio began whispering to each other. Blax looked
up, smiled and held out a remote control.

"Our government doesn't want you to have this tech."

Drixilio nodded. "You wouldn't believe how cranky they are."

"The short of it, Bertie-man, is yes. You can have the codes for
the bleeper."

"The what?"

"The transportal doorway-opener, which you requested."

"Really?" Butterflies of excitement scraped his stomach.

"On one condition: you are the first to come through the
doorway."

Before Albert could respond, the screen flashed black before
symbols and diagrams flashed over it at a rapid pace. Then the
signal went dead.

"Not bad, Doctor," the major said, clinking her glass with his. After the conference had wrapped, someone had popped champagne.

"What about Bobby and Chook?" he asked. "Should we negotiate for their return?"

"They're in an unfortunate situation." She sipped from her glass. "I'll have to give it some thought. But I need you clear-headed if you're going to be DAFT's first interstellar diplomat."

Albert looked around the studio. The possibility of exploring other planets was on everyone's lips. His whole life he had dreamt of doing so. And this tech would have other applications too – transport around the world would be instant. It would be a game changer in travel and freight. People could work anywhere in the world and still live in their village. Why had the aliens given it up so easily?

Major Wong said, "I've asked Sally to organise you a psychologist."

He winced. "Honestly, Major, I'm fine. I don't have a problem."

"Sharing is the first step."

Across the room, Sally was laughing with a technician. The atmosphere felt festive, although Albert didn't. The pink eyes would soon be relaunched and the codes that had streamed down would be deciphered and built into the interstellar transportal bleeper. Albert knew the technological leap from this would be astounding. But he couldn't help thinking they had been tricked.

He excused himself through the crowd, slipped out of the room and down the corridor, glancing back over his shoulder. Grace and the aliens were probably having a debriefing right now. He opened the door to the soldiers' change rooms where several clear-eye suits were hanging. He'd prove they were up to something.

12

IN A DARK SECLUDED corner of the bar, Bobby wiped his chin and looked back at the glamorous crowd. God, he really hoped none of the frogs had seen him puke. Under the table, the rancid stench from his rainbow splatter wafted up. He held his breath and tried arranging a stool over the top of it in an attempt to hide it. This is such a fail, he thought. The first bar he'd been allowed in and he was going to get kicked out.

He glanced over at Chook happily chatting to that cranky frog, the one who had shouted at everyone. Now Chook was acting like he was his new BFF.

Bobby rearranged the stool one last time before swaying back to their table. His gut was a sea of suffering. Cranky frog gave him a stink eye and strutted away.

"We've gotta bail," Bobby said, looking over his shoulder at the bar where wrinkly frog-barman was serving cranky frog. No one had spotted his puke yet. "We gotta get back."

"He's fucking hot," Chook whispered.

"What?"

"Zojax." Chook nodded towards the cranky frog at the bar.

Bobby winced. "Him?"

"I'm gonna ask him if he's..." Chook looked at ceiling, thinking. "You know, into blokes. I'm pretty sure he is. Gay-dar never lies."

"Mate, he's another... species. You don't even know if he's male."

"Don't do this, Bobby. I was very supportive when you had a thing for Ms Jacobs."

"Yeah, but that was before I knew she was a space frog."

"Albert went there."

"He's an idiot. And I'm sure he didn't know. You can't do it with another species."

"I can't believe this." Chook's eyes were wide and earnest. "The shit you're talking is what used to get people like me locked up. Bobby, love is wherever you find it."

"And what if you're in love with a horse?" Bobby held on to the table for balance. "Say, for instance, the most handsome pony trotted through that door. Would you wanna, you know, ride it?"

"Don't be stupid. A horse can't communicate. A horse can't describe the beauty of what it is to be alive, not like Zojax." Chook smiled, looking back at the cranky frog.

Bobby tried to focus on his hand. Could that rancid gloop let him communicate with a horse?

"We're just two beautiful intelligent beings," Chook continued. "That will hopefully explore a relationship."

Bobby swayed. "Remember that time we got stoned in old McKenzie's paddock? You were feeding his horse grass and, man, did that stallion have a thing for you. I'm talking a massive..." He stretched out his arms wide.

"Shut up, Bobby. You're drunk."

"And frogs, they have tiny little..." He held up his pinkie finger.

Zojax stepped back up to the table and placed three drinks on it. "What're you guys talking about?"

"Nothing," said Chook.

"Actually," said Bobby, as he fumbled with his trousers. "We were talking about something very big."

Chook put his hand over his eyes, cringing. "Please don't."

"We were discussing this." Bobby placed the broken remote control on the table. The room seemed to be turning on an axis. "Any idea where we can get another?"

"A bleeper." Zojax picked it up and looked it over, his big bug eyes squinting. "This one appears to be long range," he said, frowning at the geometric lettering on its side. "It will be difficult to replace. Its destination has been custom-programmed."

Bobby noticed the barman wandering near his strategically placed barstool. He shoved the remote back in his pocket. "We should go."

―――――

Chook and Zojax took the lead down the glistening corridor, both laughing at one of Chook's lame jokes. Bobby followed at a distance. He didn't trust this Zojax. For all he knew, he could be kidnapping them.

As Zojax weaved them through the space station via a series of slick white corridors and slimy-mouth doors, Bobby felt completely lost. He leaned against a fleshy throbbing wall. The ceiling also pulsed. Everything looked the same. It was like they were inside a giant glow-worm.

Bobby watched the two of them happily chatting ahead and felt a dark mood come over him. They seemed too happy. Chook could end up staying here and marrying this guy. And then who would he hang out with?

Years ago, when Chook had transferred to St Helens High, Bobby had been a bit of a loner. The whole school knew who Chook was though, because the principal had gone over the top at assembly, hoping the kids would make him feel welcome. Everyone wanted to know Chook, the funny mainland kid whose parents had died in a car accident and had to move down from Sydney to live with his gran. He knew about all kinds of cool city stuff like lattés, sushi and hairless cats. Then Chook had sat next to Bobby in class and asked if he smoked pot and they'd been inseparable ever since. Now this frog-dick was going to ruin everything.

As the air became warmer and mustier, and the corridors tighter, Bobby noticed more and more wall tattoos scribbled over the glistening surfaces. They were definitely heading into the wrong part of the glow-worm, he thought. Two little frogs barged past, chasing each other and Zojax stopped in front of a mouth-door. "This is it."

"I can't wait to see inside," said Chook.

I can, thought Bobby.

The door yawned open and they stepped into a small room with a little window and a shaggy couch that could've been made of moss. Bobby looked around, the fleshy walls had all been tattooed with massive pictures of planets, fists and bold geometric text. It looked like a highway underpass.

"I know it's not much, but it's home."

"I think it's beautiful. And very cool," Chook said, sitting on the couch and rubbing his hand over the moss.

"So," Bobby said, "What's this business about a show?"

"Don't get me started," Zojax said, plonking himself beside Chook. He pointed at the tattooed walls. "We're doing a protest campaign to cancel their stupid show. I hate it. It has no respect for intelligent life, or the intelligence of its viewers. They harass the local inhabitants and make them do ridiculous things."

Bobby said, "I want to see it."

Zojax looked at him with what Bobby assumed were serious eyes then clicked his fingers. Bobby wasn't completely sure, what with Zojax being a green frog, but he thought he sighed. The wall started to bulge towards them forming a circular bubble, wiggling.

"I hate this thing," Zojax said. The bulge suddenly split apart exposing an eyeball behind it, the wall wrinkled up like a tattooed eyelid.

Bobby said to Chook, "Are you getting this?"

Chook held up his phone.

The eye on the wall blinked several times before misting over into a viewing screen.

"Oh my god," said Chook, "that's Doctor Albert."

Bobby saw Albert sitting behind a desk talking to two alien frogs. "What the hell?"

Albert said, "We humans have been studying the cosmos for eons. We. as a species are—"

"Blah, blah, blah," the alien woman said, waving her hand. "Try harder, Bertie-man."

As Albert argued with the aliens, Zojax turned down the sound. "This is the weekly episode where they talk with some chosen idiot."

"So it's not a documentary." Bobby looked at Zojax.

The alien smiled sympathetically and explained no one was interested in studying Earth, or any other primitive culture, for that matter. "I'm sorry." He shrugged his skinny shoulders. "But it's true. We've already studied loads. And, surprise!" He gestured with his hand. "It turns out, they're nearly all primitive. They all have wars, worship angry gods, go dancing, destroy their environment and spend too much time and resources trying to make themselves attractive to the opposite sex."

Bobby noticed Chook looking at Zojax with adoring eyes. Chook eased himself into a position on the couch that was closer to Zojax, pretending he was making space for Bobby to sit down, and patted the empty seat.

"Nah, I'm right," said Bobby, still standing. He wanted to watch the show. And didn't particularly want to be near Zojax. The frog couldn't be trusted.

Zojax continued. "Up until recently, your Earth had been designated a nature reserve. It was strictly a non-interaction zone. Sure, some idiots would still go there to prank humans by abducting them and putting probes up their bottoms, but we mostly left you alone. The vibe was, your planet had lovely scenery, but the locals were arseholes. Sorry," he apologised again and smiled at Chook. "Then when the news our old message had finally arrived, and your ability to keep it secret was a spectacular fail, some folks were intrigued.

"Scientists weren't, and neither was anyone high up, but the media were. They got wind of it and one group was given special access, on a covert basis. They could mess with you, but they were told not to reveal too much info about us Gatogrosians."

On the screen, Bobby saw an image of himself vomiting in the corner of the bar. "That only just happened," he said.

Then the screen flicked to a mirror image of the room they were in. Bobby was standing and Chook and Zojax were sitting on the couch. Bobby waved his hand, seeing it reflected. "What is happening?"

"Bobby and Chook," a loud robotic voice said, "how are you enjoying our space station?"

"Oh no," whispered Bobby. It was the same robotic voice they had spoken to on the beach.

Zojax leapt out of his seat and reefed down the tattooed eyelid like a curtain and clapped his hands, the bulge in the wall receded back.

"I hate that thing," he said, patting the wall flat. He turned to look at them. "When I saw you both in the bar, I was sure you were in on it. With this being the highest-rating show in the universe and the fact that you're both constantly featured, I thought you were part of the publicity stunt."

Bobby's pulse was racing. They were being laughed at across the universe. He was pissed off. These bastards were taking advantage of him, Chook and everyone he loved. "We're shutting this down. How do we do it?"

"You can't. I've been protesting, petitioning our government. But it's too massive."

Bobby crossed his arms. They had to do something.

A beep came from Zojax's pocket. He pulled out a glowing screen and looked at it. "Excuse me, I have to take this," he said, leaving the room.

"Quick, look around to see if he's got a remote control," Bobby said. "We gotta get back. I'm gonna go global with this. We gotta shut down those pink eyes."

Chook smiled, still holding up his phone at Bobby. "I think he might be the one. I might be in love."

"Don't be ridiculous. You just met him." Bobby ran his hand over the slimy walls checking for cupboards, or anything where Zojax might hide something. "I don't think we can trust him."

"Are you kidding?" Chook pointed his phone at the tattooed walls. "He's so passionate."

Bobby glanced at Chook and shook his head. "Get it together. We have to return home."

"Why don't we just ask him to help us?"

"Oh sure. The fabulous Zojax is going to save us from all the bad frogs, is he? Chook, I hate to break it to you, but *he* is a frog. They all want to make us look like idiots in front of the entire universe. And we don't even know the guy."

Chook frowned, looking puzzled. He put his phone in his pocket. "You're jealous."

"I'm bloody not!"

"Bobby, he can help us."

Zojax came back into the room. "Help you with what?"

Chook said. "We have a little problem, and were wondering if you could help us get home."

Zojax smiled at Chook, sat on the couch and patted Chook's thigh. "It would be my pleasure."

Chook smiled warmly. "Thank you so much."

Bobby groaned.

"Are you ill?" Zojax asked.

"Probably." Bobby stared at the tattooed wall. This wasn't going to end well. Earth was going to shit and Chook was falling in love with the enemy.

Chook said, "Show him the bleeper again."

Reluctantly, Bobby handed it over.

Zojax took it and clicked his fingers. A stone coffee table rose slowly from the floor.

"Oh my god," said Chook, as he shuffled his feet out of its way, "that's amazing."

"Yeah, wow," muttered Bobby sarcastically, "our minds are blown." With everything they had seen, Chook was acting very awestruck by a coffee table.

Zojax clicked his fingers again and a box rose out of the coffee table. "And this is my toolbox," he said, opening the lid and pulled out a square looking piece of glass.

"Very impressive," said Chook.

Zojax placed the remote on the table and held the glass over it. "Your bleeper is set to two destinations. Here and your home."

The glass in his green hand glowed, geometric writing flashing on it as he slowly waved it above the broken bleeper. The remote popped open. Inside, a tiny glowing crystal with circuitry around it pulsed.

Even in Bobby's slightly nauseous state, he could not help but be impressed by the astonishing sophistication of this. They were not only light-years from Earth, they were light-years ahead.

Zojax took out another tool that looked like tweezers made of laser beams. With very delicate green hands, Zojax used them to adjust the crystal a tiny fraction. The circuits began to glow. "That should work." He sealed the remote again with a wave of his glass and from his toolbox, took out some black sticky tape to stick down along the crack.

Bobby said, "You're millions of years ahead of us in technology, and you still use sticky tape."

Zojax smiled. "All done."

"We should test it," said Bobby, taking the bleeper into his hands and examining the taped side. The tape had somehow melted in and he could see no trace of it. The crack was sealed. He pointed it at a wall, pressed the button. An electric hum began. The air in the room stirred and the glowing blue doorway they had seen before flickered into existence. Through the blue light,

Bobby could make out the shapes behind it. It looked like a living room. "Nice."

Chook clapped his hands. "Oh Zojax, you're fantastic."

Then the doorway fizzled into a static hiss, flashed three times and crackled into nothing. The hum stopped. The smell of burnt electrics permeated the air.

"Oh dear," whispered Chook.

Bobby tried the button. The doorway sprung up again, glowing blue and humming for five seconds, before it spluttered out into static and vanished.

Zojax said, "It appears it has trouble maintaining a connection."

"No shit," said Bobby. "Have you got another one?"

"Not for this destination."

Chook sat up, his eyes wide. He looked from Bobby to Zojax. "What happens if you get stuck" – he swallowed – "between doorways?"

"Every atom which makes you will be spread across the universe like a smear of glitter. To put it mildly, you'll cease to exist," said Zojax.

"Bobby" – Chook folded his arms – "Let's stay a little longer."

"But we have to save Tasmania. And the Earth."

"We can send them a text. A big one. Very informative."

Bobby rolled his eyes. "Don't be a—"

"I'll come with you." Zojax interrupted and stood up. He held out his hand to Chook. "Together, we'll take the jump."

Chook smiled, took hold of his green hand and also stood. "You'll have to meet my gran. I'm sure she'll love you." They looked into each other's eyes.

Bobby groaned. God, this was going to be one seriously long-distance relationship. "Now the doorway only stays up for a few seconds. If we mess up our leap, we're toast." He held up the remote. "Ready?"

Zojax said, "I think it'll be safer if we go separately. You first. And then I'll go with Chook."

Bobby looked from Zojax to Chook, who had a big smile on his face.

"Don't worry," Chook said, squeezing Zojax's hand, "we'll be fine."

Bobby's jaw set firmly. "You had better be." He didn't like that Chook was trusting his life to the sticky tape fix-it frog he'd only met two hours ago. He could be smeared into glitter across the universe. But who was Bobby to stand in his way? This was what Chook wanted and it might be true love after all. He handed the remote to Chook and said, "I'll see you on the other side."

Chook nodded and clicked the button. The doorway sprung up and as he jumped for it he turned to see Chook leaning in to kiss Zojax. Then everything turned to light.

13

THE YELLOW BEAMS of the wagon's headlights cut through the fog as it puttered up the gravel street. The only thing that would assuage Albert's feelings of suspicion was taking matters into his own hands. He'd prove Grace was an alien. Exactly how, he still didn't know, but he would try.

He pulled onto the grass edging the road and killed the engine. The car spluttered out of life. He cranked up the stiff handbrake and eyed the house across the street. It looked like a picturesque suburban home: white bricked with a leafy garden. Obviously, the perfect hideout for an alien headquarters. Her lights were on, illuminating the plants outside her windows. Brilliant. She must be home.

Was he a fool for attempting this? If Grace was an alien spy, she might be dangerous. The major had no idea he was here. She, Sally and the soldiers were all back at headquarters, clinking champagne and high-fiving each other. They completely believed he'd convinced the aliens to give them their tech. But Albert knew the frogs were scheming. He'd had no choice but to lift a clear-eye suit off the rack.

The car door creaked and he swore. Gently, he closed it behind him and slapped the button on his chest. He held out a hand in front, gazing at the spot where it used to be. Only the gravel road was below. He was completely transparent. He waved his arms around, still not seeing them. This suit was fantastic. Just to make sure he was still solid he touched his belly button.

As he slowly started towards Grace's house, he felt disembodied as if his mind were floating in space. Still, he could hear his feet crunching the gravel. Bloody hell, that's noisy, he thought. He started walking on his tiptoes. The crunches became softer.

Grace and the aliens on the TV might be plotting the downfall of the human race. It wasn't going to happen on his time. He was risking his life to get proof to show Major Wong. She'd see he wasn't some drug-addled idiot.

A shadow shifted in the kitchen and he stopped. Was that Grace? He hid behind a tree, peeking around. Was she in her alien form? As she stepped into view he breathed out a foggy sigh of relief – she looked human. Quickly, he waved away his foggy breath so she wouldn't notice. God, she made jeans and a t-shirt look glamorous. The first time he'd met someone he really liked and Major Wong would probably dissect her.

She's not human, he repeated to himself. He shouldn't think of her as a person. She was an alien. And what happened to her after he'd proven she was one wasn't his problem. Plus she probably wasn't anything like he had first thought. As far as he knew, everything she had done was an act. She was a militant spy, who would probably murder him if she knew he was on to her.

As quietly as he could, he stepped through the garden, picking his way between shrubs towards the kitchen window. Under his shoe, a stick snapped with an enormous crack. "Shit," he hissed, holding dead still like a statue. His breathing sounded deafening. She can't see me, he repeated. I probably just sound like a possum.

At the window, he peered inside. Grace was standing at the kitchen bench, cutting up carrots. She still looked gorgeous. Not at all like an alien. His breath started to fog up the glass and he wiped it clean. As he watched her, he realised making dinner wasn't really an act of ultimate aggression. But then alien invaders probably needed to eat too.

She turned to put the carrots in the microwave and glanced up at the window, stopping mid-step. Their eyes met. She looked right at him. Panic started to rise in Albert's throat. It's okay. Just relax, he told himself. You're invisible. She's just looking out the window.

"Albert? Is that you?"

"Fuck!" He squatted into the bushes. Shit. Shit. Shit. Had he accidentally turned off the suit? No, his hands were still invisible.

Above him, the window slid up. Grace popped out her head and peered down. "What are you doing there?"

Again, Albert held up a hand in front of his face to double-check. Right in the spot where his fingers should've been, he could see Grace staring down at him. He was definitely transparent.

"Albert? Are you alright?"

Just keep still, he thought. His blood bubbled with fear. She can't see me.

"Albert? What are you doing?"

She sounded angry. Keep still. She'll go away.

"Albert. This isn't normal."

Was she going to murder him? She probably had a ray-gun that would zap him into a bug, that's what frogs eat, isn't it? "Nice night we're having," he said.

"You've got sticks and leaves all over you. Do you want to come inside? I could make us a cup of tea." She had a worried expression on her face.

Slowly he stood. He looked over his shoulder at his car. Maybe he could make a dash for it. But... the answers, there'd be none if he ran. "Yes, a cup of tea would be lovely."

"Then come through the front door like a sane person." Grace slid shut the window with a thud.

He disentangled himself from the bushes and waded through the leaves and branches to the front door. His heart pounded. Was she onto him? She couldn't know that he knew she was a space frog, but being invisible definitely wasn't going as planned. Maybe this particular suit was faulty. He checked his legs. He still couldn't see them. His whole body was transparent.

The front door swung open. Grace stood there with her arms crossed. Between her eyes sat a little frown.

Panic rose in Albert's throat. Act like this is normal, he thought. "Hi," he managed to say, pulling a stick out of his hair.

"I didn't think you were the type. I expect this kind of thing from my students. Not from the guy I'm dating."

"Um... I'm not sure..." he began. She seemed so normal. His mind was racing. "How can you see me?"

"Come inside, you idiot."

He followed her into the living room. He hadn't been here since the night he witnessed her in her true alien form. The night he'd been thinking about for days. It was much the same as he remembered it: couch, lampshade and a big-screen TV, which had the news on it. Melbourne Storm had just won their first game of the season. The smell of cooking permeated the room from the kitchen. It wasn't at all like an alien base. He asked again, "How is it you can see me?"

"I'll put the kettle on." She left him to sit on the couch in front of the TV. "Do you have milk?" she called.

"Please."

Grace came back into the room, carrying two steaming mugs. Albert swallowed nervously and took one from her with a shaky hand. "Oh, that's lovely," he said, taking a sip.

"So," she asked, sitting next to him, "are you going to tell me why you were hiding in my bushes?"

"Well," he began, "I'm here because you're..." He took a deep breath. He could do this. Just hit her with it. "Because you're an alien."

"I'm an alien," she repeated. Her eyebrows shot up. "Why would you think that?"

He looked at where his hand should've been holding the mug.

He knew it was trembling, but he couldn't see it. Was she going to kill him? "Well, how else can you see me?"

"Oh, Albert, you sad man. You think I'm seeing you because I'm an alien? I agreed to see you the other night because I thought you were nice. But, now I'm not so sure."

"I don't mean dating." He shook his head. She had it all wrong. "I mean seeing-seeing. With your eyes. I'm invisible."

She looked him straight in the face. "Really?"

"Yes."

"Invisible?"

"Transparent like the air."

"I'm having a little trouble believing you."

"Forget it." He needed a different strategy. He looked down at his lap, seeing only the couch below. Clearly, this suit wasn't working properly. It must have a glitch that made it invisible only to himself. Another thing he would have to explain when he got back to headquarters. "I also think you're an alien because I saw you as one the other night."

Her eyes went wide as she sipped her tea. "While we were having sex?"

"Well, yes. You flashed green, but also afterwards. Right here in front of the TV."

"I see. On the night we vaped together?"

"Don't do that. I know what you're going to say." He was sick of people telling him he had a drug problem. "It wasn't the pot. I know what I saw."

Grace looked concerned. "I'm very worried about you, Albert. Have you told anyone else?"

"Only my boss."

"What did she say?"

Albert sighed. He knew where this was going. "She said I should talk to you."

She was silent for a moment. "Anything else?"

He didn't want to say this. He swallowed. "And that maybe I should see a psychologist."

"Albert, I like you." She paused. "Well, I did before all this... creepy stuff. And if you're going to go crazy, I don't think we should see each other."

"I suppose, you're right," he said, feeling silly. Had he hallucinated it? Drugs did always affect him strangely. She was a lovely person and he was ruining whatever chance he ever had with her. It was only now he realised how much he liked her. He probably did indeed need counselling.

"But if we do continue to see each other" – she took a big sip of tea, swallowed and looked straight at him – "you must never talk to anyone about this again."

His heart jumped with hope. He might still have a chance with her. "About you being an alien?"

She nodded over her tea.

"Are you?" he asked.

"I never denied it. Sorry I suggested you were crazy."

"What?" Albert's eyes went wide. "You admit it?"

"Yes. But if you tell anyone it could be very dangerous."

"You admit it! You're an alien." He stood up. He wanted to dance. Take that, Major Wong. She could shove her drug-counselling program up her arse. He wasn't messed up. Grace *was* from outer space. "That's fantastic news!"

She smiled.

In that moment, Albert found it hard to believe that this beautiful woman was in fact a green frog with sharp pointy teeth. And that if he was lucky she might continue seeing him.

Grace stood up. "I've got to pop out quickly, but I want you to wait for me."

"Wait? Where are you going?" He began to stand. "There are so many things I want to ask you."

"We'll talk when I get back. I won't be long."

From her back pocket, she tugged out a remote control. It was just like the one he'd seen in the video Bobby and Chook posted on social media. She pointed it at the wall and pressed the button. An electric hum filled room, then a glowing blue doorway appeared. Albert stared at it wide-eyed and amazed. That was an actual traversable Einstein-Rosen bridge? Right there. How were they powering it? How did they stabilise it? He had so many questions. Through the doorway's glowing light, he could see a corridor on the other side.

"I'll return soon." She stepped through the doorway and it vanished. The hum stopped and he sat back down in silence.

A dog was barking outside in the street.

Goddamn it, he thought. She had tricked him. He sighed, knowing he would never see that beautiful alien again. It was like in high school when Clarissa Miller had said she liked him and wanted to meet up after school. He'd stood in the middle of the oval, turning in every direction, hoping to see her coming, checked every seat in the grandstand. It was dark and had started to rain when he trudged home. The next day, the whole school was laughing about it.

He may have discovered for certain that Grace was an alien but he felt empty, lost. Only just before, when they were talking, had he felt that they really had something. She was the calm to his manic. He hoped she would come back. Or would she just be another Clarissa? He looked at the space where the doorway had been.

And he still didn't have any actual proof. Though there might be one thing. He'd have to search her bedroom for the device they'd used to smoke the other night.

Suddenly, the hum started again and the doorway reappeared, bathing the room in pulsing blue light. Butterflies tickled his stomach. She hadn't tricked him.

Albert held his breath as the doorway pulsed. A body tumbled through and landed face first on the carpet, groaning and dressed like Albert was in a black invisibility suit. Then the doorway hissed into static and vanished.

"I think I'm going to puke." The figure rolled over and clutching his stomach.

Disappointed, Albert recognised Bobby. "Where have you been?" he asked. "Everyone's been looking for you."

"What the fuck?" Bobby stumbled to his feet, looking around in fright. "Who said that?"

"Right here." Albert tapped his chest.

Bobby jumped. He had the face of a wombat in headlights. His hands were up, and he started backing away. "If that's the soldier I kicked in the balls, I'm sorry, okay? It was stupid."

"Bobby," Albert said, slowly. "Can you see me?"

"Doctor Albert?" Bobby's eyes darted around the room. "Is that you?"

Albert wanted to tear his hair out. Grace could see him, but Bobby couldn't. God, this suit was so frustrating.

Albert slapped the button on his chest and materialised.

Bobby took a quick step backwards. "Fuck, Doc. Don't do that to people."

Albert muttered, "I guess it does work."

"Doc, we've got to stop the aliens. They're totally fucking with us." Bobby looked at him with wild eyes. "Why are you wearing an invisibility suit?"

"Never mind," Albert said quickly. "More importantly, where have you been?"

"Doc, you wouldn't believe what we've seen. Absolute next level. Space stations. Aliens. But not just space frogs, space bears too. And grasshoppers."

Albert's eyebrows shot up as words vomited from Bobby's mouth. He described the weird wet fleshy walls on the space station, the doorway remote with its crack – Chook's fault, apparently. "And there's this disgusting gloop that you drink." He sucked in a breath. "It lets you talk to aliens in any language." Breath. "And then we discovered the space frogs are not making a documentary."

"That's right, it's actually a scientific study of us in our natural environment."

"No, Doc!" Bobby shook his head. "They're taking the piss. They're making a reality show. It's the biggest in the universe."

Albert leaned back on the couch, sceptical. But then he considered all the mockery he received from Blax and Drixilio, being put in a situation to have sex with Grace, and her tricking him just then. He rubbed his hand over his chin. Had they planned it all?

"Bobby, you must come with me. We'll need to debrief Major Wong. Do you still have the portal device?"

Bobby looked back at the spot where he'd dived through. "Chook should be through any minute. He's got it and loads of proof on his phone. We filmed everything. Their whole space station, the bar, everything."

Bobby waved his hand through the air where the doorway should have been. "C'mon, Chook. Where are you?"

Albert watched him, wondering if Grace would be next to jump through the doorway. He wished to the stars he'd been smarter and kept the whole alien thing to himself. Would she appear at all? Even though, in his heart, he knew the aliens were tricking them he still hoped she'd come back and that they might work out a way to be together, despite all this. Why did he always hope? He had hoped people would understand the first message from outer space. He had hoped this experiment would change the world for the better. Was he still that nerdy boy waiting on the oval? At the time he knew it had been the wrong move to wait so long. Had it been hope that made him stay? Or was it cowardice? Desperation? If he'd left earlier, he wouldn't have been the butt of those humiliating jokes.

He said to Bobby, "We'll wait five minutes."

They both sat on the couch, looking at the spot where the doorway had been.

14

SATURDAY

BOBBY SQUINTED, half awake, trying to see what was making that awful noise. His whole body ached from sleeping sitting upright. Next to him on the couch, spread out with his eyes shut, head back, was Albert, snoring louder than a walrus who'd smoked a pack of cigarettes.

Last night, they'd spent hours waiting for Chook. Albert had desperately tried to convince him to see his boss at DAFT, saying, "Bobby, I'm very sorry, and I do know how you feel, but I don't think your friend is going to appear. Major Wong will know what to do." Bobby had refused, saying, no way he was going anywhere. Best mates don't leave. They don't let each other down.

Outside the window, the sky was turning from black to blue. A pink eye floated past, watching. Probably broadcasting me to aliens right now, Bobby thought as he raised his hand and saluted it with his middle finger.

Obviously, Zojax had betrayed them. When he saw that frog, he'd punch him in the face. Chook had to still be alive. Bobby just had to figure out how to get back to the space station. Maybe Ms Jacobs had another remote hidden somewhere.

He rubbed the sleep from his eyes, feeling a lump of dread form in his gut like he'd swallowed a bucketful of mucus. Shit was going to get real if he couldn't get Chook back. Really real. The cops would think he was responsible for Chook's disappearance. There'd be a secret trial, waterboarding, and he'd spend the rest of his life in Guantanamo Bay being the pet of some massive terrorist. Chook's gran would be devastated. The only people who would believe that he'd lost his best mate in outer space were Albert and the idiots he worked for. The very people in charge of this stupid experiment.

Think, think, think. If he was going to get back and save Chook, he needed to be invisible. Then he could infiltrate the space station without anyone knowing. All he had to do was fix this stupid suit. Quickly he tapped the button again, hoping, but nothing happened.

Albert shifted on the couch, snoring.

The doc's suit was still working, Bobby thought. He'd seen him materialise last night. Quietly, he stood up. He didn't want to wake the doc, because he knew he'd stop him and drag him back to see his boss, but he had to get that suit off him. Slowly, he walked up to the doctor. Albert's chin was pressed into his neck, covering the zip of his suit. With the gentlest of hands, Bobby touched Albert's stubbly chin and lifted his head. With his other hand, he slowly unzipped the suit. As it pulled it down, each set of teeth made a soft click.

"Oh god." Bobby winced. Albert was naked underneath. He continued to unzip him, trying not to see any more than he had to. He exhaled with relief when he saw Albert's yellow underpants.

Albert grunted and moved.

Bobby froze for a moment. When Albert had settled, Bobby gently, eased out one of Albert's arms, then slid out the next. Then he shuffled off the trouser half. With the suit in hand, Bobby undressed, slipped on Albert's suit and zipped it up. He slapped the button on his chest to check the invisibility worked and then hit it off again. Now for the doorway remote, he thought.

In Ms Jacobs' bedroom, he crept past her neat bed to a chest of drawers. Last time he'd come in here, the remote had been sitting on top. Surely she had another one. He slid open the top drawer, trying not to make any noise. It was full of underwear. That's a lot of lace, he thought as he patted his hand through them, feeling for anything like a remote control. Then he felt it, something long and cylindrical. Yes, this was it. He knew she'd have another one. He'd be rescuing Chook in minutes.

He shoved all the underwear aside and his eyebrows shot up. Ms Jacobs, you naughty lady. He really hoped it wasn't what it looked like, but was actually a space-door remote. Carefully, he lifted it out and hefted its weight. The long silver device with its bulbous head had geometric writing down the side. It was definitely space-frog tech, but it looked a hell of a lot different from the last remote he'd stolen. He checked it for buttons and found a small one on the bottom. This was it, he thought hopefully, then pointed it at the wall like a remote. He was going to open another doorway and rescue Chook. He pressed the button, holding it down.

In his hand, the device glowed bright like a glowing sword.

No doorway appeared.

"Come on." He pressed the button.

Again it glowed bright, bathing the room in a soft glow, but no doorway materialised.

"Fuck!" He stared down at it, wanting to hurl it across the room. It was just a space dildo. A small puff of smoke was coming out of the top. Was it broken?

Then he heard it. The electric hum. His heart began pounding with excitement. No way! It had worked. He'd opened a space door.

"Chook, I'm coming."

He looked around the room, but there was no light. Only the hum. He listened closer. The sound was coming from the living room. Quickly, he ran back to the spot where he'd dived through last night. A blue doorway flickered, filling the room with pulsating blue light.

Bobby stopped, confused. Why had the doorway appeared out here? He stepped towards it. Who cares? All he had to do was jump through it.

Albert continued snoring on the couch like a walrus.

This was it. Bobby took a deep breath, braced himself and sprinted towards the door. He was going to rescue Chook. He'd get his best friend back. As his back foot left the ground and his hand outstretched, a head travelling in the opposite direction slammed into him. The head was followed by a torso, some arms and legs, and another head.

Bobby flew backwards and hit the floor with a thud. He turned to see distinctive red hair beside him. Chook groaned on the floor, holding his stomach. Bobby felt a mix of emotions rush through him: angry and glad at the same time.

The other figure picked himself up and dusted off his clothes. He was tall with a chiselled jaw, his body lean and muscular, and better-looking than any bloke Bobby had ever seen.

The doorway fizzled out of existence, leaving the slight scent of old boiled socks.

The tall man reached down to Chook. "You do get used to it eventually. I promise."

"Thanks, babe," Chook said, taking the man's hand and pulling himself up. They kept holding hands and stood smiling at each other.

"Where the hell have you been?" hissed Bobby. He pointed at the tall guy with his glowing stick. "And who the fuck are you?"

Chook's face lit up at Bobby and then frowned. "Why are you holding that?"

Bobby looked at the glowing cylindrical device in his hands. "I was going to use it to get you back."

"How?" Chook glanced at the sleeping doctor. "And why is Doctor Albert naked?"

Albert grunted, mid-snore and reached down to scratch his balls.

Chook's eyes went wide. "Have you two been..."

"Of course not!" Bobby shook his head. "He's just naked because... never mind." He pointed the space dildo at the other man again. "Who is this?"

"It's Zojax," Chook said and reached up to brush a bit of dust off Zojax's otherwise perfect hair.

Zojax smiled with perfect teeth.

Chook said, "I helped him with his disguise."

Bobby frowned. The frog looked hotter than the sun, sexier than any movie star. "It's not realistic. No one looks that good."

"Not true. I used my phone collection of hot-dude pics for inspiration."

"So he's a barbie doll," muttered Bobby.

"I think he's very handsome." Chook kissed him on the cheek.

"Thanks, babe." Zojax smiled.

Bobby rolled his eyes. What was next, matching lap dogs? Albert shuffled on the couch, still snoring. The pink eye was also still floating outside the window, filming them. "Have you got that footage you took on the space station? We're going to shut down this whole thing."

"No. I think I've had enough of this, this... journey," said Chook.

"Dude." Bobby stared at Chook. "What are you talking about? Those bloody frogs..."

Zojax coughed. "Gatogrosians."

Bobby glared at Zojax. He was responsible for Chook being missing for hours. "Sorry. Those *arseholes* are laughing at us across the universe."

"I'm going home, Bobby. Gran will be worried sick."

Zojax nodded. "Family is important."

Still snoring, Albert lifted one leg, farted then dropped the leg.

Bobby shook his head. Zojax was really starting to annoy him. "Chook, we have to stop—"

"Don't push me, Bobby." Chook put his hands on his hips. "I've already gone to another galaxy with you. And we nearly got stuck there. Besides, we're already going to be in a shitload of trouble. And the government will still want their suits back."

Bobby considered this for a moment. His mum would probably be losing her shit too about his whereabouts. "I'm not leaving you again. We have to see this through. We have to save the world. And we gotta get high."

"Fine," said Chook. "But I'm going to speak to my gran first."

"Okay, but before we go, I wanna give the doctor a present." He walked over to Albert on the couch and slipped the space dildo into his hand. Chook held up his phone and clicked a photo.

———

The pink eye floated in the morning sky behind them. Chook's small fibro house stood on a tree-lined street where the grass ran straight onto the bitumen. This is totally a waste of time, Bobby thought. They had to figure out how to shut them down.

Chook said to Zojax, "She might seem a little strange, but she's really very nice." He slid the key into the lock and swung open the door. "Gran?" he called. "I'm home."

The living room walls were painted baby pink, and a bright pink blanket covered the couch. Lining the walls were framed posters of seventies disco bands, some of them signed, one of them from ABBA. A mirror ball hung from the ceiling, spinning sparkles around the room.

"Gran? Are you about?"

"She's probably gone shopping," said Bobby. "Let's go."

Chook shook his head and led them into the kitchen. Beside the kettle stood an old lady wearing a bright-pink flannel dressing gown with bunny slippers. She had pink rollers in her grey hair and music-buds in her ears. Soft sounds of dance beats could be heard as she bopped up and down.

"Gran!" Chook said, loudly.

She turned and gasped. "Oh my god!" She grabbed Chook and hugged him and kissed his hair. "Montgomery! Where have you been?"

"Montgomery?" Zojax asked Bobby.

"Only his gran calls him that," said Bobby. "It's his real name."

Chook's face was buried in her dressing gown, as he said, muffled, "We took a trip and got stuck out of town."

She pulled back from her hug, stopped the music on her phone and looked at him with narrow eyes. "You haven't been taking acid, have you?"

"No, Gran. You know I only vape. We literally went somewhere."

"Shame." She shook her head. "I wouldn't mind another walk on the wild side." She hugged him again. "I'm glad you're home, Montgomery." She looked over her shoulder at Bobby. "You should be ashamed of yourself, taking my boy for so long."

"I, ah..." he stuttered. Why was this his fault? "Well, we would've been back sooner, but these guys had something to do." He pointed at Zojax. "He was the one who made us late."

"And who's this handsome fellow?" Gran asked, her eyes going up and down Zojax, lingering on his biceps. She touched her curlers and smiled.

"Zojax." The alien extended his hand. When Granny Adams went to shake it, he kissed the top of her hand gallantly. "A pleasure to meet you."

Gran giggled. Bobby rolled his eyes again.

"We met in a bar," Zojax said, "on the space station."

"The space station! Sounds like a nightclub I used to visit." Gran's eyes narrowed again. "Have you boys been in Hobart?"

"No, Gran," said Chook, "I would never without permission."

"We just went to another galaxy," Bobby said and excused himself. From the bathroom he could hear Chook trying to explain that going into outer space wasn't actually travelling very far. Sitting on the toilet, Bobby pulled out his phone and scrolled to his mum's number. She would definitely be worried. She'd always had mega-anxiety attacks over him disappearing. When he was a little kid, he would sneak off into the bush and his mum would go nuts, ringing everyone she knew in search of him. When he returned, she'd say she wasn't angry but very disappointed. "Bobby, you have to be a responsible boy and tell me where you're going."

He listened to the phone ring. She was going to be seriously angry.

"Bobby? Bobby? Is that you?"

"Sorry. I should've called."

"We've been looking everywhere." He could hear her voice was strained with concern.

"Mum, don't stress. I'm over at Chook's place."

"We've been so worried. Where have you been? The police are looking for you. Even the military are looking. It's very odd. What's going on, Bobby? No one is telling us anything. Are you in trouble?"

"Sorry, Mum. I won't be home for a little while longer."

"Bobby Tucker, you come home right now!"

In his gut he felt an empty hole of despair opening. Disappointing his mum was something he had done a million times, but this felt different. He really wanted to do what she said. She would probably make him a cup of warm chocolate milk. It had been a long day and he'd travelled to another galaxy and back. At that moment, to go home, even to one of his mother's lectures, seemed like the most wonderful thing in the world.

"Bobby? Are you there?"

He wasn't a little boy anymore. A single tear fell from his scrunched eyes and ran its way down his cheek. He wiped it away.

He had responsibilities. He had to save the world. "Just know that we're okay. I'm okay."

———

It was mid morning when the three of them arrived at the caravan. It felt like ages since they'd left Baz at DAFT.

Bobby hammered on the caravan. It shuddered as he did. "Baz, wake up."

A groan came from inside.

"C'mon. It's urgent." He banged again.

Baz's face poked out the door, squinting in the light with his neat sideburns and pencil-thin moustache. His eyes flicked over the three of them, lingering on Zojax. "You boys are in big trouble. I shouldn't be talking with you. You lost me my job."

"Sorry," Chook said. "I tried to talk Bobby out of taking these suits."

Baz crossed his arms.

"C'mon, Baz," said Bobby. "Let us in."

"Is that Tucker?" came another voice from inside.

Bobby swallowed. It was the same voice that had screamed his name across the schoolyard. Right before the voice's owner gave him a kicking. Bobby touched his eye where his shiner had been.

Baz whispered, "My sister has finally broken up with him."

"Oh," said Bobby. Now there were a zillion places he'd prefer to be.

Baz smiled, thin-lipped. "If you can get rid of him, then you can come on in."

Bobby sighed as the three of them tromped into the cramped caravan. Zojax had to duck his head.

Dave stared up from the kitchen table with glassy red eyes. He crossed his massive arms and gave Bobby an intense slow nod.

"So," said Baz, taking out his phone. "You're all adults. Play nice." He scooted around the table next to Dave and typed a text into his phone, ignoring everyone.

Dave glared at Bobby. "I should call the cops. They questioned me for hours 'cos of you."

Bobby looked at his sneakers. That wasn't his fault.

"They reckoned I might've done something to you."

Bobby could still remember Dave's meaty knuckles smashing into his face. The crunch they made connecting. "Did you tell them how lovely you'd treated me?"

"Piss off, Tucker. You deserved it."

"So, guys," said Chook, in a happy voice, "this is my friend Zojax. And he's lovely."

Dave grunted. Baz looked up from his phone, smiled and shook Zojax's hand.

The alien started to lean down to kiss Baz's hand but Chook pulled him back. "That won't be necessary."

"Listen, Dave," Bobby said, sitting down at the table. "You know, me and Kitty aren't a thing. We never were."

Dave leaned over the table. His breath smelt like stale bong water. His big finger poked into Bobby's chest. "You kissed her."

"And you smashed my face in." Bobby stood up, readying himself. "You should be apologising to me." He wasn't going to take this anymore. He'd travelled the universe and survived. That took balls and guts. And now this prick was trying to own him. Fuck Dave and his bullshit. Tasmania needed him. The world needed him. He was a hundred per cent confident that if he got into a fight with Dave again, he would cop another kicking. But he was willing to do it because standing up to arseholes, whether they came from outer space or Earth, was the right thing to do.

"Dave," he said, "you get one chance in this life. Don't waste it being a dickhead. If Kitty doesn't want to be your girlfriend, so fucking what. Get over it. Find another girlfriend and, next time, be a better boyfriend. We're all fucking learning here. None of us are experts in this bullshit called life." He paused and looked at Dave who was still staring at him. It was hard to tell whether he was listening or raging. Bobby wasn't sure where that speech had come from. Anger had flooded out of him. The words were his, but they didn't sound like him, or maybe they sounded like someone he might become if he survived all this.

Slowly, Dave stood up. The low ceiling made him stoop. He looked down at Bobby. "I will fuck you up."

Bobby wasn't backing down. "Yes, it was a mistake to kiss Kitty. But I fuck up all the time. I probably will again."

Chook smiled. "Oh, yeah. One hundred precent he will."

"C'mon, mate," Bobby said, reaching to shake Dave's hand, "let's put this behind us."

Dave looked at his hand then turned and stepped out of the caravan. The door slammed.

"That went better than I expected." said Chook.

Bobby breathed out a big sigh. He was sure a future kicking from Dave was on the cards, but first he just had to save the world. "Baz, can we get some fucking pot?"

A beep came from Zojax's pocket. He pulled out his slim piece of glass, reading the strange geometric writing on it.

"I gotta take this," he said, standing up.

"Nice phone," said Baz. "Is that the new Samsung?"

Without answering, Zojax stepped outside into the sunshine.

"He's cagey," said Baz.

"He's fantastic," said Chook.

"Very dodgy," said Bobby, getting up to follow Zojax. He didn't trust that frog. This was the second mysterious phone call he had received.

"Are you going somewhere?" asked Chook.

"I just wanna see if Zojax is alright."

"No, you're not. You're going to spy on him."

"Well, who's he talking to?"

Chook glared at him. "You can never be happy for me, can you?"

Bobby looked at his friend as he went to open the door. He really did want Chook to be happy but this was bigger than a little fling. "It's not like that. The guy is from another planet." God, he just wanted things to go back to normal.

Before Bobby could open the door, it swung open. Kitty poked in her head and exhaled heavily. "I thought Dave would never fuck off."

Bobby felt pangs of irritation. She wasn't the one who had punched him in the face, sure, but she was responsible for telling Dave what had happened between them. She stood in the doorway, smiling at him. Should he follow Zojax or talk to her? As she stepped inside, the door swung shut and they were standing close.

Kitty's bright eyes darted over his face. "Glad to see there's no lasting damage."

Squeezing around the table to make space, her thigh touched his leg. He tried to move out of the way, but there was nowhere to go.

"Where have you been?" she asked.

"Outer space."

She laughed, her blue ponytail bouncing as he touched his shoulder.

Bobby watched the door, wondering who Zojax was talking to.

"Baz, can we just get that pot?" he asked.

"Fine," said Baz, looking up from his phone. He reached up to a cupboard above the table and rummaged around.

As he did, Kitty reached under the table and squeezed Bobby's leg. "I didn't mean for you to get hurt. I just wanted to break up with Dave. It was a dumb way to do it."

"Sure." Bobby nodded. Now he knew their kiss didn't mean anything to her. Was that supposed to make him feel better?

Baz plonked a little baggy on the table filled with green buds. "That's my last one. Twenty bucks."

"Can we get it on tick?"

Baz's lips went tight under his thin moustache.

"You know we're good for it."

Kitty said, "If they don't pay you back, I'll give it to you, Baz."

Baz sighed and nodded.

"Thanks, Baz. You're a really good mate." Bobby quickly

scooped up the baggy and slipped it into his suit. He could always depend on Baz. Now they had to get the hell out of there. They had a lot to figure out. He started to stand. "Kitty, could you hop out of the way?"

"Where are you going?" she asked.

"To get high and save the world."

"In that order?"

A heavy knock shuddered the door. "Open up. We have you surrounded. Bobby Tucker and Montgomery Adams, come out with your hands up."

Bobby looked out the window. Armed soldiers were standing around the caravan. "Zojax," he said, glancing at Chook, who had tears in his eyes. "The frog bastard sold us out. I knew it."

Baz smiled, holding up his phone. "Fuck off, Bobby. That was me."

15

ALBERT AWOKE FEELING SORE, disorientated and bleary eyed. All his muscles were stiff from hours on the couch. He blinked at his bare legs and yellow underpants. What happened to my clear-eye suit? He couldn't recall taking it off. The last thing he remembered was waiting for Chook.

Bobby! He sat up. Where the hell was that kid? They needed to see Major Wong. He looked around, and then his eyes clocked Grace, cross-legged in the armchair, watching him, looking as beautiful as ever. She had that small frown between her eyes.

"You came back!" he said, overjoyed. Happy emotions tickled him as if he were a jar full of butterflies. "I can't believe you came back. I thought you were gone for good."

"You went through my underwear drawer." She nodded at the object in his hand.

What? he thought, confused, glancing down to see what he was holding. In his grip rested her long, cylindrical vaporiser that had got him high on their night together. He dropped it like a hot sausage.

"I never..." He shook his head. How had this happened?

"It appears you did."

The blood drained from his face. His mind raced. Shit. Shit.

He would eradicate that little bastard, Bobby. If that kid had killed his chances with Grace, he would do something drastic. He would have a quiet chat with his parents.

"Albert." Grace smiled, tight-lipped. "Don't touch my stash."

He slumped back into the couch. Last night, Bobby had shown up wild-eyed, telling him strange tales about space stations and the aliens' ulterior motives. "Grace, what's the truth?" he asked. "Are you studying us? Or is it something else?"

"Studying might not be the right term."

"What then?"

She grinned and flicked on the TV, revealing an image of a caravan surrounded by soldiers with guns. In the middle of them stood Bobby and Chook with their hands up. Oh, dear, thought Albert, this was not going to end well. Grace used the remote to turn up the volume.

"Take it nice and slow," a soldier said. "No one needs to get hurt."

Bobby glanced at Chook with worried eyes.

"This is so good." Grace's smile widened and reached down and picked up her vaporiser. "I can't wait," she said, inhaling. "We're building up to the climax." She laughed out a cloud of vape.

Albert was shocked at her level of schadenfreude. Sure, a couple of minutes ago he'd wanted revenge on Bobby, but only to get him in trouble with his mum. These schoolboys were in a dangerous situation, they could be shot, and Grace appeared to be exhilarated. She seemed suddenly very inhuman.

"Do you want some?" She offered her device.

"No. It doesn't agree with me."

"Suit yourself, but it improves my show."

"Now listen," Bobby said on the screen. He lowered his hands, holding them out in an attempt to placate the soldiers. "There's a lot more going on than you guys realise. I know for a fact the aliens are up to something. And it's not what you think."

"This is gonna be good," said Grace, smiling. "I hope they shoot him."

Albert swallowed. "Are you some kind of actor in all this?"

"Ha!" She laughed. "Actors know nothing. I'm the producer."

His eyes went wide, his stomach tightening. "Are you in charge of all this?"

"Well, yes." She glanced momentarily at him before looking back at the screen. "Except for Hextor from the network. I don't want to talk about that bastard."

The screen cut to a close-up of Bobby's hand as he touched his chest. Instantly, he vanished.

"Bobby!" Chook and Albert said at the same time.

"What the ..." yelled the soldier. "Everyone fan out."

"This wasn't the plan," Chook said with tear-filled eyes. He stood, glancing around, holding up his hands.

"Don't let him get away." The lead soldier strutted towards Chook.

The boy smiled back sheepishly, saying, "I'm sorry about pinching your suits."

With the butt of the gun, the soldier hit him hard and sent him flying backwards. Chook's head cracked on the ground with an audible thud.

"No," whispered Albert. "They're hurting him."

"Bobby! Help!" Chook cried, squirming underneath the soldier who had knelt next to him and flipped him over before reefing Chook's hands behind his back and cuffing his wrists. "You can't touch me. I'm a minor."

The soldier said into his radio, "One of the perpetrators has been neutralised."

"Ooh, Bobby is such good talent." Grace clasped her hands together. "That invisibility suit was a genius move. Go, Bobby."

Albert was feeling sick when his phone vibrated in his pocket. Major Wong's number flashed up. "I have to take this."

Grace's eyes remained fixed to the screen.

"Hello?"

"Doctor," Wong barked. "Where the hell are you?"

On the TV, Chook was being shoved into a van. "Somebody call my gran," he yelled. The door slammed shut.

"I'm talking with Grace, as you suggested."

"We need you back here. A-SAP!"

"Why? What's happened?" He already knew. She was going to gloat to him about the capture, but he couldn't let on he already knew without giving up Grace.

"Operation Leapfrog is a go."

"Huh?" He had no idea what she was on about. Albert squinted, trying to think back to everything the major had told him in the last couple of days. There had been so much. "What does that mean again?"

"It means, you banana, that our interstellar transport device had been built. The prototype is complete. And we're ready to take the jump."

Albert looked at Grace, who was smiling, delighted at the events on the screen. Was this also part of her plan? How much of it had she orchestrated? He whispered into the phone, "I think we should call the experiment off."

"Doctor, please plug your brain back in. This is a giant leap for the Australian government. I want you back here within the hour." The phone beeped as she ended the call.

Uncomfortable anxiety was creeping up Albert's throat like a rash. On the screen, they were following the van, watching Chook looking forlornly out the window.

Grace was laughing on the couch. "This is brilliant," she said. "I couldn't have planned it better."

Albert stood up in his yellow underpants, his muffin-top belly protruding over his waistband and looked around for something to wear.

Grace looked at his underpants. "You going somewhere?"

"Work." He shrugged, apologetically. Would this be the last

time he ever saw her? Who knew? The way he was feeling, it might be for the best. She might plan to do something to him as well. "Grace," he said, "I know things aren't exactly going perfectly between us, and I apologise about your vape device. But your secret is safe with—"

"Albert." She stood and put a finger on her lips. "Shut up."

"No, I need to say this because if I don't, I'll hate myself later." He paused, trying to think of the right words. Grace had a hungry, intent look in her eyes. Was she going to kill him? Or worse, eat him? "I don't—"

Grace rushed at him. Albert gasped. He raised his hands in fright. She slid an arm around his bare neck, and lowered his hands with her other. Albert breathed nervously as she stepped in close to his face.

"This couldn't have gone more perfectly," she said.

"I guess."

"Kiss me, Albert."

She pressed her lips into his. Her mouth was warm and moist as he gave in. She might be the most beautiful alien on the planet, but she was beautiful in the way a lion was, completely deadly.

Their kiss held for almost a minute. When Albert opened his eyes, he noticed a pink eye watching from outside the window. Was this part of her plan?

———

Albert stepped into the reception area of DAFT's headquarters. He could see a pink eye floating in the reflection of the automatic glass doors. Was Grace still watching? Excitement bubbled in the room. Soldiers were standing around, chatting with each other. They weren't even invisible anymore. Albert glanced around, wondering where they were detaining Chook. The poor kid was probably being questioned. In their way, those boys had tried to do the right thing.

Major Wong strode up to him with a smile on her face. "Doctor, I'm glad you decided to turn up."

"Apologies for my tardiness." Albert shrugged. "I was sort of in the middle of something."

"Not performing for the pinkos, I hope." The major laughed and slapped his shoulder. "So is she an alien?"

"Who?" he asked too quickly.

"The schoolteacher?"

"Oh." He laughed, nervously. His mind was racing through the possible answers. If he told her about Grace being an alien again, the major would think he was more than a rampant pothead. She might start to question his sanity. "We kind of just, you know, talked it out."

"Good for you, Doctor." She nodded, quick and curt. "I'm happy to tell you, we've captured one of the delinquents."

"I know."

The major's eyes narrowed. "How?"

He couldn't say he'd witnessed Chook's apprehension unfold on Grace's TV. "I overheard on the way into the building."

The major grunted. "Well, we've got bigger fish to fry, Doctor." She explained the technicians had been extremely excited to receive the codes from his last videoconference. "They've built a prototype overnight. Outstanding work, Doctor."

"We should take some more time to consider our options."

"Don't be a chicken nugget. It's ready. And you're going through."

Albert had seen how enraptured Grace was with her show. He didn't want to be the aliens' entertainment. "Opening an untested Einstein-Rosen bridge here could be catastrophic. It might destroy Tasmania. Or the planet."

"We fired it up this morning and it's fine. Even threw a test subject through on a string."

"A human?" Albert swallowed thinking about the unfortunate soldier who had to endure the risk to make sure the doorway was safe.

"No, a cabbage."

Blood drained from his face.

She continued. "And we dragged it back. No damage."

"But," he said in a soft voice, "I'm not a cabbage." His life and others shouldn't depend on the success of a vegetable. "My human biology is completely different."

"Actually, we share ninety-five per cent of the same DNA. Doctor, your aliens built this thing to transport sentient beings. It's safe." She gave a sharp nod. "And the cabbage came back extra fresh. I made a lovely salad with it."

He couldn't do this. He wasn't trained to go on covert missions. No one knew anything about the terrain on the other side. He was a scientist, not someone who did things. "But, I'm not—"

"Doctor, you're going through in three hours. The grunts will follow. This is part of our deal with the aliens. You're to be the first. That was *their* stipulation."

Albert felt the floor shift under him. Was he going to faint?

She looked at him and laughed. "The Gatogrosians wouldn't suggest you go if it was dangerous." She paused and her eyes narrowed, serious. "We need more tech, Albert. Don't piss them off."

He wanted to tell her that the aliens weren't studying them for a documentary, he wanted to tell her about Grace and anything that would stop this disaster from happening.

"Doctor, you're going to be very famous after this."

He already was, he thought, and he hated it. Fear churned in his stomach. When he'd first discovered the aliens, he'd been so excited about the idea of being famous and winning accolades, he'd stupidly broadcast it and it had nearly – no it *had* – ruined his reputation and he'd lost his job as an astronomer. This was a mistake. Another stupid mistake. He was meant to be studying the stars, not going to them.

"Doctor Manning, you are going to change the world." Major Wong put her arm over his shoulders and began walking him towards his office. "It won't be me, or Sally. Nor those idiotic delinquents. It'll be you. You'll represent our whole world. Your planet needs you."

Albert winced.

16

DESPITE THE THROBBING ache in Bobby's hands, he wouldn't
risk climbing down. Not yet. He'd been clinging to this branch
like an invisible koala for too long to give up. Below him, the last
three remaining soldiers and Baz climbed into a van.

"Thank fuck for that," he whispered as they drove off. He
began to pick his way down the tree. It seemed like those freaks
would never leave.

Bobby hadn't planned on abandoning Chook, he'd panicked
and slapped the button on his invisibility suit as the soldiers had
closed in. The tree in the middle of the yard was an easy escape
and he'd climbed as fast and as quietly as a possum. Under him,
Chook was screaming for his help.

The gumtree had presented him with a perfect and awful
view. Bobby had hated watching Chook being shoved into the
van. He'd had to squeeze his eyes shut and grit his teeth. He'd
break Chook out as soon as he could.

Climbing down as the wind blew gently in the leaves, he saw
Zojax creeping back. Bobby watched the good-looking alien slip
into the caravan. What the hell was that frog up to?

He dropped onto the ground, steadied himself and stepped
up to the caravan. He was going to confront that sell-out

bastard. The door swung open. Kitty and Zojax were sitting around the small table. The handsome alien was holding his hands together, appeared very worried. Kitty was puffing up a joint.

"Bobby!" Kitty cried. She stood up, smiling. "You're back... and you're... totally pink."

Bobby hit the button on his chest and materialised. "It's a side-effect of the pot. It allows you to see the invisibility suits." He stepped over, plucked the burning joint from her fingers, and sucked back a deep toke. The smoke was harsher than his vape, but he held it down. As soon as he exhaled, he felt his anger and fear beginning to ease.

Kitty said, "Baz was really pissed off about losing his job. He'd been moaning about it for days."

Bobby glared at her. Was that some kind of apology? "Did you know he was going to sell us out?"

"Don't start with me, Bobby." She glared back with big eyes, raising herself in her seat. "You stole those suits and got him fired. He was doing you a favour, selling you pot at his work. He was trying to go legit. And you fucked it for him."

Bobby looked down at his suit. They *had* stolen them from Baz's workplace.

"Mum and I are sick of you idiots banging on his caravan door. We want him to go straight and back to university next year." She looked away and bit her bottom lip, her eyes down. "No one wants to be known as the drug dealer's sister." She glanced back at Bobby, shaking her head. "But no, I didn't know he was going to do that."

He nodded. He didn't know anything about Baz wanting to go straight. He'd never mentioned it, but he believed her. Bobby turned and stared daggers at Zojax with his sexy smug face. "What's your deal? Where did you go?"

"I had to take a phone call. When I saw the guns, I hid."

"Pretty convenient timing."

He glared back at him, fiercely. "I hate to break that little ego, but I'm organising a protest movement back home. You're not the only species being exploited."

"Bobby." Kitty held up her hand. "Don't fling shit at everyone. Neither of us had anything to do with Chook being taken away. It was because you stole their suits, plain and simple. It's no one else's fault."

Zojax nodded. "And I'm more at risk than you too. If they catch me, they'll dissect me."

Bobby took another drag of the joint. He couldn't take Zojax seriously, he was too annoyingly good-looking. "Can't you transform into something more realistic?"

"Chook likes this." He tapped his chest.

"He's not here."

"And whose fault is that?"

"Fuck off."

"Both of you chill," said Kitty, taking back the joint and sucking a hit. She exhaled. "Just relax."

"No," Bobby said. "This shit has to stop." He glared at Zojax. "We're going to rescue Chook and shut down the pink eyes."

Zojax scoffed. "I want him back as much as you. But how? Those armed soldiers don't seem happy."

Kitty nodded. "I don't fancy being killed either."

"Actually," Bobby said, "I have an idea."

———

"This has to work," Bobby said, staring at Zojax. "It's all we have."

Zojax looked at Bobby with concerned eyes. "There's a chance it could go wrong. You might get stuck."

"I don't care. We're doing this."

The three of them were in a car park, behind a building, not far from DAFT. When they'd left the caravan, Bobby had turned his invisibility suit back on and together they paced the streets, glancing over their shoulders, to make sure soldiers weren't following them. Whenever they saw a glowing pink transparent soldier on a corner, looking out for Bobby, they turned the other way. It took hours, with lots of detours, but eventually they'd reached the other side of town. Zojax pulled out his remote control. It looked different to the one Bobby had stolen. It was more square with a screen.

Bobby asked, "Have you got it set to the picture?"

"The one we took this morning? It's good to go."

Kitty asked, "Can I do it?"

Zojax handed her the device and showed her which button to press.

Kitty stepped in close to Bobby. "Are you ready for this?"

"No. But I can't think of any other way to get Chook."

She pressed the remote against Bobby's forehead. "Last chance to back out."

He felt as if he was about to be shot at point-blank range. "Do it."

Kitty clicked the button.

He groaned as pain stretched and twisted through his muscles, pulling at him everywhere. It stung worse than when he'd stacked his bike on gravel. It was all over his body. He gritted his teeth as he felt his mouth begin to change. His teeth and gums warped. His nose expanded. "Arrgh!"

"Oh my god," said Kitty, puffing his vape. "This is trippy."

The transformation stopped as suddenly as it had begun. Bobby stretched out his limbs as if he were about to go for a run. Not so bad, he thought, feels okay. The pain had completely subsided and he was feeling normal again. He touched his face. Stubble covered his chin, much more than had previously been there. His hair felt wiry and messy, his stomach flabby. "How do I look?"

"Just like him."

Bobby went up to a parked car and pulled out the side mirror. In the reflection, Doctor Albert Manning looked back at him. "Next fucking level!"

"I'll do myself," said Zojax, and held the remote to his head.

His body began to warp and change shape. A few seconds later Zojax appeared exactly like Bobby.

"Very handsome," said Kitty and squeezed Zojax's shoulder. "Firm too." She turned and winked at Bobby in his Albert form. He had the rather awkward sensation of seeing Kitty flirt with him, who wasn't him. It was like an out-of-body experience.

"I'm sorry, Kitty. You can't come in with us," said Bobby.

"Are you kidding me? Why would I want to? Those soldiers have proper guns. I wouldn't go if your life depended on it."

"Then you'll stick to your part of the plan?"

"Of course. I want to save the world too."

———

Bobby waved his hand in front of the automatic doors of DAFT. They didn't open. He waved again. Still closed. Inside behind the reception desk, he could see a woman working on a computer. He tapped the glass, waving at her. She pointed to the intercom on the side.

Bobby took a deep breath to ready himself and pressed the button. Then said in a deep voice, "Hello, I am Doctor Albert Manning."

Zojax hissed, "Don't adjust your voice. Just talk naturally. You'll sound just like him."

"I got this," Bobby hissed back. "You don't have to school me."

"Right. You're doing marvellously."

The intercom squawked, "Doctor, where's your access pass?"

"Oh, you know me. Super forgetful," Bobby said, still putting on his deep voice. "I must have left it at home."

Zojax was glaring at him. "That was terrible."

"Shut up."

"Alright, Doctor." The intercom squawked.

The doors slid open and they stepped into the building; armed soldiers lined the room, watching him. Fear beat a rhythm in Bobby's chest. This was it. Make or break. The moment of reckoning. If he got caught here, it was all over.

The receptionist stopped him. "Is your pass on your desk?"

"Oh no," Bobby said, quickly. "I'm pretty sure I left it at home."

"But you came in an hour ago."

Bobby shrugged. He didn't want to get caught on the first obstacle. "I went home for lunch."

She looked at him over her glasses, with a stern gaze. "Doctor, this is a high-security facility. You must keep your pass on you at all times. I will give you a temporary pass this once. It will work only for today. Bring it back with your proper pass tomorrow."

One of the soldiers stepped up to him. "Doctor Manning, sir. We'll take this individual to the holding room."

"No." Bobby waved his hands, shooing away the soldier. "I can manage this little guy. He's turned himself in." He smiled at Zojax. "You're not going to cause any problems, are you?"

Zojax shook his head, glaring at the soldier.

"We *must* escort you, sir."

"Oh no you don't." Bobby stepped between Zojax and the soldier. "You're not stealing the credit off me."

"Sir?"

"I captured him all by myself. I don't want your help. Thank you very much."

The soldier looked confused.

"So where's Chook at?"

"Chook?" The soldier frowned.

Bobby rolled his eyes. "Montgomery Adams."

"The other offender is being held in room 3C."

"Thanks, bro." Bobby gave Zojax a little shove along, while saying, "C'mon, you little perp." They headed down the first corridor Bobby saw. He had this, he thought. This was too easy.

"Doctor," the soldier said, trotting behind them. "I must escort you with the prisoner."

"Fine," Bobby said and shoved Zojax forward again.

As they walked ahead, Zojax hissed, "If you push me one more time, I'll use the bleeper to transform you into a bug."

He's a bit grumpy, thought Bobby. It was weird watching himself; it gave him a strange dream-like sensation. This copy of himself wasn't quite right. Sure, the image was perfect, but there were subtle mistakes. For one, Bobby thought, his walk was much sexier than this frog's version. He carried himself with so much more swagger.

"Doctor Manning!" called a loud voice.

Instantly, Bobby wanted to duck and hide behind Zojax. A woman in military uniform was striding towards him. He knew she was Albert's boss from the town hall meeting and when he'd been called into his office.

"Excellent work catching the other delinquent."

"Yes," said Bobby, using his deep voice again and patting Zojax shoulder. "He turned himself into me. I'm just locking him in with the other one."

She stepped up close and stared at him. Her eyes narrowed, assessing.

Bobby swallowed, thinking, there could be no way she knew. She couldn't. I am Albert. I am Albert.

She whispered, "Doctor, you're not stoned again, are you?"

"Not a chance," Bobby lied, out of habit. He always lied whenever anyone asked that, particularly his mum.

"Well your eyes are red, your voice sounds odd and you're acting weird."

"Nah," he said. "I never do drugs."

"Don't be a banana. You admitted it to me the other day."

Albert smoked the green? Who knew? He didn't think the old mate had it in him. "What I meant to say is I don't do them anymore."

"Well, you're acting very strange."

"I guess I'm just happy I caught this guy."

"Good work," she said. "Put him in the room and get ready for Operation Leapfrog. We launch in one hour."

"Anything you say, lady. I've got this totally nailed."

"Doctor." She stared hard at him. "I know these are stressful times, but I want your mind on the job for the jump. Straighten yourself up."

Before Bobby could respond, she turned and marched away.

"Totally nailed?" Zojax hissed as they walked ahead of the soldier. "What was that?"

"You told me to talk normally."

"I said your voice would *sound* like him, I didn't say speak like an idiot."

"Whatever."

The soldier led them to room 3C. Bobby used the temp access pass to swipe the lock. It beeped and remained closed. Bobby tried it again. Still closed.

"Apologies Doctor." The soldier stepped forward with his access pass. "This is why I must escort you." He swiped it and the door buzzed open.

The soldier stepped in first and the other two followed.

Chook was sitting slumped in a chair, his face was bruised and his hands were behind his back with his wrists handcuffed to the chair.

"Chook!" Bobby said.

Chook lifted his head up. "Doctor Albert, could you please call my gran?" Then his eyes flicked to Zojax and his face drained of hope. "Oh, Bobby. They got you too."

Bobby turned to the soldier. "That will be all."

"Doctor, I must remain with you in the cell."

"Really, not necessary."

"They're my orders."

"So I'm giving you new orders."

"You can't, sir."

Bobby shook his head. "Thought you might say something like that."

Behind the soldier, Zojax held up the remote close to his neck and zapped him with his remote.

"Arrgh!" He dropped to the floor as his body began to warp and remould, slowly shrinking smaller until a pile of clothes lay on the ground.

Bobby swallowed, nervously. "Is he dead?"

"Of course not. I'm not a murderer."

"What'd you turn him into?"

"A potato."

Bobby nodded thoughtfully.

"Hello, sweetheart." Zojax stepped towards Chook. "We've come to rescue you."

"Bobby! Oh my god. I knew you'd come." Then he frowned. "Why did you call me sweetheart?"

"I'm Bobby," said Bobby.

"What? You're Doctor Albert. He's Bobby."

"No," Zojax said. "He's Bobby."

"Really?"

"Yes," said Bobby, "as Doctor Albert."

Chook looked at Zojax-as-Bobby. "Then who are you?"

"I'm in disguise, babe."

Chook turned from one to the other with a look that made a stunned mullet look like Einstein.

Bobby said, "We used his transmorpher."

Chook, still glancing back and forth, finally nodded and said, "So, Doc, you're Bobby and Bobby, you're Zojax?"

"Nailed it."

"Am I still Chook?"

"I certainly hope so."

"I'm sorry, Babe," said Zojax as he walked up to him. "I know how much you liked my other look, but this was the only way to rescue you. I'll be back to my old self, or my new self, soon."

"I don't care," he said, looking up into Zojax's eyes. "I know it's you. Just kiss me."

Bobby watched himself lean down and plant his lips on Chook and winced. It was like watching himself kiss his brother, if he had a brother, or kiss his mum. Admittedly, Chook had good taste in men, but really, just gross. "C'mon, we've got to get out of here."

Zojax pulled out the glass device that he'd used for his phone calls and to analyse their broken bleeper on the space station. He stepped behind Chook and waved it over his handcuffs. It bleeped, Zojax glanced at it and pulled out his laser tweezers from a pocket. "Don't move, sweetie." He pointed the lasers in the lock. The handcuffs clinked open.

"Thank you," said Chook, rubbing his wrists. "I can't wait to go home. I need to have a nice hot bath."

"Not yet," said Bobby. "We're moving onto stage two."

"Hurry up," Bobby said, as Chook struggled to pull up the trousers of the soldier's clear-eye suit. "You're taking forever. We could've totally saved the world by now."

Chook rolled his eyes and continued to tug at the legs.

Bobby went over his plan again. It felt solid in his head. Everything was going sweet. He looked exactly like Dr Albert and Zojax looked exactly like him. They had managed to rescue Chook. And Zojax assured him that he could easily shut down what he called the primitive pink-eye tech. Once that happened, they'd leg it through the blue doorway to Zojax's place on the space station where they'd chill for a couple of days. Too easy. That is, if they ever got out of this room.

"Chook, c'mon."

Chook slid his arms into the suit. "I'm not really feeling the vibe on this, Bobby. Perhaps we should just head home. These people are seriously pissed off with us."

"Are you cray cray? We're gonna cop it whether we do this or not. So we might as well. All we've gotta to do is sneak out there and find the pink-eye broadcast room. And besides..." He held up the soldiers security ID, dangling on a string. "I've got a VIP pass."

Chook raised his eyebrows. "That's your plan?"

"Well, mostly."

"It sounds lame. And every time we do something you suggest, we end up in more poo. If this keeps going, we're gonna drown in it." He paused, looking at the potato on the ground. "Look at that guy. He's a vegetable because of you."

"Actually, your boyfriend did that."

"Sorry, babe," Zojax said. "Do want me to transmorph him back?"

"No," Bobby said. "He stays a vegetable. We don't need a soldier going apeshit. Chook, this is the last thing. Then it's over."

Chook looked at him. "I'm tired of doing everything Bobby wants. My suggestion is we go back to my place and binge watch TV with Gran."

"Babe," Zojax said in a gentle voice, "we're in this now. Together. We have to see it through. No one will get hurt."

"No one *else* will get hurt, you mean."

Bobby nodded. "And I promise when this is over and we hang out, we'll do whatever you want. Play video games, go to the movies, whatever."

Chook looked down. "Should we take him with us?"

"Who?"

"The potato."

Bobby looked at the potato on the floor and tapped it with his shoe. It was white with a few pockmarks and blemishes. It looked remarkably like a potato. "Why? Do you wanna make some chips?"

"Bobby, think of the bigger picture. He might have a family."

"And you think they'd like a potato?"

Chook zipped up the front of his suit. His face wore a worried expression. "I just want to know if he will be alright. I'm not a murderer."

Zojax shrugged sympathetically. "I imagine for a potato, he will have a very nice life."

Chook scowled at them both.

"Fine." Bobby sighed, picked up the potato and tossed it to Chook. "You're carrying him." In Doctor Albert's body, Bobby went to the door and peeked out. "The hallway is clear. C'mon."

Chook whispered, "These people are going to kill us."

"Shut up, Chook."

They stepped into the corridor and they crept single file, with Zojax at the rear. Bobby opened the first door he came to and looked inside. It was a stationery cupboard. He sighed and snuck along to the next door. This one looked more promising as it had a security access panel beside it. Bobby swiped his pass. The mechanism made a loud click as it unlocked. He swung open the door. The room had three desks with computers and a filing cabinet.

"This has to be your dumbest plan yet." Chook folded his arms. "We'll never accidentally stumble onto some pink-eye broadcast room."

"Would you stop being so negative?"

"No, I'm positive. This plan is shit. It's shit-tastic."

"Be quiet," whispered Zojax. "Someone is coming."

They turned to see Baz walking down the corridor. "Fuck!" said Bobby. What was he doing here? He should be back at his caravan getting stoned. That douche had sold them out. Bobby wanted to punch him in his stupid little moustached face.

"That's it," said Chook, "we're busted. And to be honest, I'm glad it's over."

"Play it cool," said Zojax. "Bobby, remember, you're Doctor Albert. You're just taking us somewhere for interrogation."

"Baz," Bobby said in a deep voice as the rat-faced, pencil-moustached, traitor walked towards him. "Good to see you. Can you help me out for a sec?"

"Doctor?" he stopped. "What's wrong with your voice?"

"Nothing," Bobby said quickly.

Baz looked at Zojax-as-Bobby and Chook. They glared back.

"So," Bobby asked, "have you got any clue where they're broadcasting the feed from those pinkos?"

Baz eyed him strangely and Bobby swallowed. If this didn't

work they'd have to turn Baz into a vegetable. But then, the snitch would deserve it.

"Doctor Manning, I'm doing your make-up in there in half an hour."

"Correct answer." Bobby laughed in his deep voice. "I get so confused in this place. So many rooms. So many doors." He rolled his eyes. "You know me, Doctor Fuddle-brain. Where is it exactly?"

"Down the corridor to the left," Baz said, dryly. "There's a sign on the door saying broadcast studio. Are you alright?"

Behind Baz, Zojax lifted the remote towards Baz's neck.

Bobby's eyes went wide. He shook his head, hissing, "No."

"You're not okay?" Baz looked concerned. "What's wrong?" He lowered his voice. "Is it those two?"

Zojax continued to point the remote.

Bobby shoved Baz into the wall.

He squealed as he bounced off and landed on the floor. "What the hell are you doing?"

Bobby stood over him and pointed. "You should be ashamed of yourself. Bobby was your friend. What's wrong with you?"

"I don't understand. I was only doing what you guys told me to."

Bobby glared at Baz, looking up with nervous eyes and his pencil thin moustache. "Well," Bobby said, feeling sorry for him. "Don't do it again." He strode away, pushing Chook and Zojax up the hallway. "Come on, you two."

Zojax turned and hissed, "Why did you stop me?"

"How would I explain that to Kitty?" Bobby hissed back. "I'm sorry, but we turned your brother into a potato."

"He's going to be suspicious. I could've turned him into a bug."

"Like that'll improve my chances with her."

Chook whispered, "Personally, I think you have zero chance with her. But I also don't think we should turn anyone else into a potato." He paused. "Or a bug."

"Shut up, Chook."

"I'm serious." He protested as they walked on. "Zojax, give me the transmorpher. I'm going to look after it."

As the alien handed it over, they came to the door marked *Broadcast Studio*. Bobby swiped his pass. The lock clicked open and they stepped into a dark room.

17

IN THE STAFF KITCHEN, Albert poured hot water into his cup. A lovely cup of tea would fix everything. If one thing could turn around a horrible situation it was a nice cup of tea. This was the calm before the storm. The moment before a star goes supernova. This might be the last cup he had.

He was shaking off the bag when the make-up guy came into the kitchen. Baz looked at him with a pale face and wide eyes. The kid could use some make-up himself, Albert thought.

"Doctor?" The kid looked over his shoulder then back at Albert. "What are you doing here?"

Albert frowned. "What does it look like?" He held up his cup. "This is meditation. It calms the soul. Did you know Carl Sagan was a big tea drinker as well?"

"But you were just in the corridor. You pushed me over."

"Really? That doesn't sound very nice." Albert took a sip. Lovely. That sweet taste of relaxation. "You must have me mistaken for someone else."

"You shoved me right into the wall."

"I did not."

"I'm going to HR!"

"I haven't touched you." Albert glared at him. This kid was ruining the tea experience. "Perhaps you need a glass of water."

"How did you get in here so fast?" He looked nervously around the kitchen. "And where are Bobby and Chook?"

Albert's eyebrows shot up. "Bobby?" The last time he'd seen Bobby was on Grace's TV. Soldiers had surrounded him and Chook and he'd used his clear-eye suit to vanish.

"Yes, Bobby," Baz said slowly. "You were just with him."

"I assure you I wasn't. I've been in my office."

"Then... how?" Baz glanced over his shoulder and back at Albert. His face was even paler. He appeared skittish. "It was you, just like you."

"Like me?"

Baz nodded anxiously. "Bad hair, needing a shave and a little pot belly. He even had your face."

Albert winced. Something was clearly going on. "Are you positive it was me?"

"A hundred per cent."

Albert sipped his tea, thinking for a moment. Bobby had wanted to shut down the pink eyes. If he was receiving help from someone or something... This could be trouble. "Where did they go?"

"The broadcast studio."

"Right." Albert downed the rest of his tea. "We need some soldiers."

18

BOBBY-AS-ALBERT FUMBLED in the dark searching for a light switch. A stage lit up at the front of the room with intense bright lights. It looked just like a TV studio. One wall to the side held a rack of monitors, each showing the footage the different pink eyes were filming in the town at that moment. Several were watching the DAFT building, focusing through the windows.

Another pink eye was in front of the stage strapped to a tripod. It looked like a hostage. This was the moment. Bobby nodded at Zojax.

"Do your thing, frog man. It's your time to shine."

Zojax-as-Bobby stepped up to the pink eye. He looked it over before poking it with his finger. The eye wobbled like jelly. Then Zojax pulled out his phone and entered several codes into the device.

Chook put a hand on Zojax's shoulder. "Babe, please tell me this is gonna work. I really wanna get the hell out of here."

"No problem," he said. "I'm going to jam the network and crash the pink eyes. Then I'm going to infect the network with an advanced virus so if they make any more, they will broadcast a frozen image. To make it work again, they'll have to reconstruct the pink eyes and reinvent the coding."

"Sounds amazingly boring." Chook kissed his cheek. "Just hurry up."

Bobby stood in front of the pink eye, squinting in the blinding studio lights. This was where Albert had talked with the aliens when he saw them on Zojax's weird TV.

"Almost there," Zojax said as he placed his phone on the skin of the pinkie and pulled out his laser tweezers. They sizzled as he pushed into a fleshy spot. He called out to Bobby. "You ready?"

"Wait a second." Bobby picked up a small whiteboard and a pen, thinking. This needed to be on the money. Since the arrival of the pink eyes so much had happened. He'd grown so much. Humans had received advanced tech that would forever alter how they lived. He needed to write something that captured the essence of the shared human and alien experience. Something that sent a message to future generations. Quickly, he wrote down: *Fuck off from Tasmania.*

On the stage, he stood in front of the pink eye and took a deep breath. "Do it," he said to Zojax. Then he held up the whiteboard and his middle finger. "Over and out."

Zojax tapped the screen on his glass phone. It glowed and the pink eye shuddered and began to deflate. The wall of TVs showing footage from all the pink eyes now broadcast the same frozen image of Albert holding up his middle finger to the universe.

"Did it work?" Chook asked.

"I believe so," said Zojax.

"Next fucking level!" Bobby yelled. "Fuck those frog bastards. They shouldn't have come here messing with Tasmanians. Fuck off back to your own galaxy." He high-fived Chook. Zojax kissed Chook. And then they all group hugged.

"You fucking legends," Bobby said, their heads locked together as if in a rugby scrum. "And, Zojax, I'm sorry I didn't trust you."

"Don't worry about it," he said, smiling.

"Nah really. You're awesome." Bobby slapped his shoulder.

"I'm glad you're with Chook. You're the best bloke he could ever hope to meet. Out of a thousand galaxies."

Chook smiled. "It's true, you're wonderful."

As they stood out from their group hug, Zojax looked into Chook's eyes and took his hand. "I'm only wonderful because of you."

"That is so beautiful." Chook put his hand over his heart.

"You're a natural at this." Zojax said, softly.

"A natural?"

"Billions thought we were perfect for each other. And you've been so great." Zojax smiled. "But I've got to be heading off."

"What do you mean?" Chook gripped tighter to Zojax's hand. "We've got so much to talk about. Don't you wanna come back to my place and chill?"

"I've finished my deal with the network. This is it, boys."

"What?" said Bobby, trying to comprehend what the hell Zojax was saying. An uncomfortable lump settled in his throat.

"I don't understand," said Chook, quietly.

Zojax glanced at the frozen image of Albert on the screen. "I suppose it's safe to say." He took a deep breath. "Viewers loved me helping you and your show gave my campaign the exposure it needed. Thank you so much." He squeezed Chook's hand. "It's become so big the network cut me a deal to finish the show and they promised to back off from exploiting other primitive cultures."

Chook snatched his hand away. "But... but what about us? You were going to show me the universe."

"Oh, baby, that was just pillow talk. I do really like you, but..." He shrugged and patted Chook on the cheek. "We had a special time. Honestly, you were fantastic in the sack."

Bobby clenched his fists. That absolute prick. He fucking used us.

A bang cracked through the room and the door to the studio flew open. All three of them turned to see soldiers running into the room with Baz and Albert following.

The doctor yelled, "Bobby Tucker. Stop what you are doing right now."

Soldiers surrounded them with rifles ready.

"Shit," said Bobby. The hair on the back of his neck stood up as he stared at a dozen gun barrels pointed right at him.

"I should be going." Zojax pulled out his bleeper.

"Fuck you," said Chook. "I hope you die."

"C'mon, sweetie, don't be like that. It's just show business."

19

ALBERT STEPPED in front of the armed soldiers, feeling rather pleased with himself. They should've known not to mess with Doctor Manning. He felt he could handle anything. Maybe even a little jaunt in the major's wormhole.

Bobby, Chook and the imposter were nervously eyeing the guns, when Albert saw Bobby slip something out of his pocket. He recognised it from the videos Bobby had posted online. It was an intergalactic transporter device. Bobby hit the button, an electric hum filled the room, wind started to blow and then a pulsating glowing blue door appeared next to them. That little bastard Bobby was planning an escape.

"Well, guys," Bobby said. "It's been real, but I've got to be going."

Albert yelled, "Remove that device from Mister Tucker."

A soldier aimed his gun at Bobby's head but seemed unsure about approaching closer to the doorway.

"Get him!" screamed Albert.

The soldier edged forward.

Bobby stepped towards the pulsating portal. "I'd love to stay for the after party." He shrugged. "But my contract clearly states

I'm only here until the end of the show. And I have a tight sched-ule." With that, he jumped in the blue light and vanished.

Damn it, Albert thought. How was he going to explain that?

The imposter and Chook looked at each other for a moment, then Chook shook his head. "No way. I'm not following that guy anywhere. And I'm over this stupid journey of yours."

The doorway blinked out of existence.

Albert stepped in closer to peer at the imposter, who had his hands raised in surrender. He couldn't believe what he was seeing. Baz had told him the man looked exactly like him, but this was more than exact. The sight was unsettling. Did he really look that shabby?

"How is this possible?" he asked as his eyes went up and down this facsimile, assessing its body and face. The stubble, the big nose, the belly. It was perfect. "I don't understand."

The other Albert glared back, mutely. Albert made a mental note: being angry makes me look rather ugly.

"Handcuff them," he said. "Before they cause any more mischief."

He turned to walk out, but stopped mid step upon seeing the wall of monitors. Every screen displayed an image of himself holding up his middle finger. Twenty screens all with him giving the one-finger salute and holding a sign that read: *Fuck off from Tasmania.*

He knew intellectually that it wasn't him on the screens, but inside his gut an atom bomb of anxiety exploded. Everyone was going to think he had ruined things. Again. "Oh dear," he whis-pered. "This is not good."

Albert turned from the wall of monitors, feeling sick and looking pale, staring back at the other version of him. "What have you done?"

"Stop it." Imposter Albert snatched his hands away from the handcuffs. "He's not the real doctor. I am." He pointed at Albert. "He's got you all fooled. He's an imposter."

Albert shook his head. This was out of control. "I don't know who he is. But he's not me."

"No!" Imposter Albert yelled, standing straight and tall. "I'm the real Albert. He's actually an alien in disguise. He's using his alien mind tricks on you."

"I *am* the real Albert. That man must be an alien."

"Stop copying everything I say."

"I'm not."

"Only an alien would say that."

Albert smiled, tight-lipped, not saying anything. He wouldn't be caught up in this idiotic game. He was an astrophysicist. No one could trick a genius. Unless, that is, the imposter really was an alien, one with a superior intellect.

The soldiers turned back and forth between the two, guns raised on both.

Imposter Albert raised his fists. "C'mon, you fake-arse alien. I'll smash you."

Albert stepped backwards in fright. "I'm a scholar not a fighter."

The imposter lunged forward, swinging his right fist and clocking Albert in the jaw. His head bounced backwards. Stars dotted his vision. Intense throbbing pain stung his face. Jesus, Albert thought as his head spun, he had never been in a fight. Why would anyone want to do this?

Imposter Albert said, "That's what you get for pretending to be me." He jabbed hard, connecting with Albert's chin. "C'mon, you alien fucker."

"Stop it." Albert put up his hands, trying to protect his head as the imposter hammered down more hits.

"You stop it." Imposter Albert jabbed. "Stop pretending to be me."

"I'm not!" Albert screamed and swung out, slapping the imposter very hard on his ear.

"Bloody hell!" The imposter staggered backwards, holding the side of his head. "You're not supposed to slap people like that."

One soldier stepped forward, shouting, "Stop it. Both of you!"

More soldiers stepped in and aimed their guns next to both of their heads. "Put your fucking hands up!"

"But I'm the real doctor," said Albert.

"Bullshit, I am."

"I can prove it."

"So can I."

"Shut up!" the soldier screamed. "Handcuff the lot of them."

"What about me?" asked Chook. "This wasn't my idea. I wanna go home."

"Shut up!"

Imposter Albert muttered, "Wish we'd turned them all into potatoes."

20

THE HANDCUFFS behind Bobby's back were too tight and hurt his wrists. He suspected the oversized gorilla who had shackled him loved inflicting pain on people. But Bobby was so angry at Zojax and Albert, he didn't care what happened to him now. At least they had shut down the pink eyes.

The three of them were marched up a corridor, surrounded by armed men, then shoved through a door into what looked like a strange laboratory. Major Wong stopped talking to an engineer as Bobby-as-Albert stumbled in. Her eyebrows shot up.

"What the hell did you do this time?"

"Um..." Bobby looked at all the technicians sitting behind computers who formed a circle around the room. What the hell was going on? There were video cameras mounted on tripods, all pointed to the centre of the lab.

Albert came stumbling through after him, also wearing handcuffs.

Major Wong's mouth dropped open.

"Major," Albert said. "Thank god. Please tell them to release me. This is a terrible mistake."

"No release me," said Bobby. "He's a fake."

"Bloody hell," she said. "Sergeant," she addressed one of the soldiers. "What is going on?"

"Major, I swear to you," Albert said. "I'm the real Albert."

Chook staggered through the door. "Stop pushing me!"

Bobby tried to think of a way out as a soldier explained the situation to Major Wong. She kept looking at him and the real Albert, her eyes darting back and forth between them, as though she were trying to discern the difference.

"Major," Albert said, "I don't know who this man is, but he's not me."

"Don't listen to him," said Bobby. "I am Doctor Manning."

"He's lying."

"You are."

The major held up her hand. "I don't know which of you bananas is real, but if you've compromised my pinkos, there's going to be hell to pay."

A lady holding a tablet stepped forward. "Major, we have another problem. Social media is going wild over this."

The major leaned over and peered at her screen. Bobby glimpsed images of himself posing for selfies with an alien in the space-station bar. Oh, Kitty, you absolute legend, he thought. Thank you for sticking to the plan. He owed her big time now because her brother would probably get trolled for a hundred years for selling them out.

"Damn it." The major turned to Chook. "You and your idiot friend couldn't leave it alone, could you?"

"I'm really sorry," Chook said. "If you just call my gran, I'd like to go home."

"Did someone hit you in the head, son? 'Cos you've gone stupid. There will be no going home after what you two have done."

Chook looked at his shoes. Bobby wished he could reach out and tell him not to worry. He was certain Chook's gran, his mum and everyone would know they were trying to save the planet.

The major glared at him and Albert. "I told one of you, those idiots would ruin everything."

"Major, I –" Albert began.

Major Wong's phone rang.

Bobby heaved a sigh of relief. He and Chook might become international heroes. They could start a YouTube channel.

The major was listening to her phone, staring at them all with beady eyes. "No, sir. Of course I haven't spoken to the media... Well, sort of. We've captured one of the two perpetrators... Of course. If you insist." She ended the call.

Bobby grinned. Obviously, one of her bosses had just given her a serve.

Albert asked, "Is the experiment into the wormhole being called off? I really think that's a good idea. The tech really isn't ready."

The major raised one eyebrow, looking at the real Albert before her eyes darting back and forth between the men again. She said slowly, "Operation Leapfrog is still going ahead, Doctor Manning."

"What? Why?" Albert asked. "There are too many variables."

"I will not have this mission jeopardised. The aliens are waiting. And we have an opportunity to establish Australia as a world leader." She nodded at the engineer. "Open the doorway."

The engineer lifted up a big device that looked like a large bleeper, pointed it at the centre of the lab and clicked the button. A low hum filled the room, wind started to blow through people's hair and the blue doorway flickered into existence.

The lady with the tablet asked, "Which Albert will you send?"

"One of them is an alien. The other is our doctor. The aliens wanted an Albert first, so they can have theirs back." She put her hand on the real Albert's shoulder and said a soldier. "Please escort Doctor Manning to the holding room."

She glared at Chook. "This one and his friend have been a pain in my arse for weeks. He's going through too."

Chook shot Bobby a look that could assassinate.

The blue doorway hummed.

"Oops." Bobby swallowed. They'd done this before. It would be all right.

"Don't do this, Major," Albert shouted as he was being shoved away. "It'll be one giant mistake for mankind."

21

ALBERT SAT on the floor of room 3C feeling extremely worried. Major Wong had made a mistake sending through Chook and whoever that other version of him was. Whatever happened next was going to be bad.

Suddenly, an electric hum filled the room and the wind picked up. Albert shuffled backwards towards the wall as a doorway fizzled before him.

Grace stepped out with her hair blowing gently in the wind. "Albert, you have to come with me."

He stared at her like she just offered him a poo. Clearly, she was insane.

"Bobby and Chook need you. Your planet needs you."

"I'm very sure I'm *not* the right person to help my planet. I've been down that road."

"But you are, Albert. You're perfect." She squatted on the floor next to him. "So many people believe in you. You just have to as well."

He looked at her. Was he supposed to swallow that?

"Two years ago," she said, "I was full of dreams and I tried to convince the network to take a punt on this long-forgotten holiday destination called Earth. You know what they said?" She held up her hand as if it were a puppet, and said in a deep voice, "You want to waste my resources on that pile of shit of a planet? Only idiots want to watch primitives." She laughed. "Well, fuck them. It's gone gang busters. And so have you. People love you, Albert. You're a superstar."

His eyes went wide. "You did all of this?"

Her phone started beeping but she ignored it, nodding at Albert. "I took a risk on this planet. On this show. And I took a risk on you. You're the best thing to come out of it and the best thing that has ever happened to me." She held his hand. "Now take a risk on me, Doctor."

———

Blue light blinded Albert's vision as he staggered out of the glowing doorway. His whole body tingled with sharp stings as though every molecule in his being had been violently torn apart, then restitched together by the universe's fastest and cheapest tailor. His consciousness returned with a jolt. Nausea washed through his gut. He pressed his hand against his belly, suppressing the urge to vomit.

As his eyes adjusted, Albert saw a glistening white corridor. He stepped closer to a wall, examining it. An opaque jelly-like substance with tiny veins of red, blue and green inside it throbbed light. His fingertips wiped off some slimy residue and he sniffed it. The wall seemed to be constructed from a similar organic material as the pink eyes.

Grace stepped through the doorway, her eyes flicking up and down the empty corridor. She took a deep breath and smiled at Albert. "You need to drink this." She held up a small bottle of glowing gloop. "It might taste disgusting but it's worth it."

"What does it do?" Albert lifted the lid, sniffed and winced.

"Translates language."

He looked at Grace. It would be incongruous for her to take him across the universe only to poison him. Hesitantly, he put the bottle to his lips. The thick sludge slid down his throat like mucus.

"Come on, let's go." Grace walked ahead.

The ceiling pulsed white light as Albert struggled to keep up with her pace. She was moving with determination and he wanted to look at everything. Out the window were stars and planets he'd never seen. He stopped at a picture on the wall that looked like it had been tattooed into the surface. It was of a circle with a fist in the middle.

"Grace, what's this?"

"A protest sign," she said, not stopping.

Grace led him through more and more corridors, until Albert started to hear chanting. Here the corridor opened into a wide room filled with Gatogrosian protestors. Young and old frogs stood holding signs of the circle with a fist, chanting at a line of uniformed guard-frogs. "*Free the primitives.*"

The crowd saw Albert and cheered.

"Bertieman, are you here to end the cruelty?"

Before Albert could answer Grace dragged him behind the barricade and around the other side of the guards. She took a deep breath and pressed a button on the side of a large horizontal crease in the wall, which then spread apart yawning open like a mouth. Drool dangled like slimy ropes around the sides.

"Are you ready?" Grace asked.

"Not at all."

Inside was a large office with massive colourful tattoos lining the fleshy walls. Albert's mouth dropped open. One was of Bobby fighting some big kid, another was Bobby and Chook baring their bottoms at a pink eye, and the last one was a kiss between Grace and him.

"Hextor!" Grace strode across the room. "We need to talk."

Hextor turned, frowning at Grace and Albert. He was sitting behind the only desk in the massive room before a wall of blinking eyeballs. He was the fattest Gatogrosian Albert had seen. He was dressed in a fancy suit, but this alien wasn't glamorous like the other ones he'd interacted with, he looked more like the toadyish Blixitor who had sent the message. This toad kept its eyes fixed on the wall of eyes: all with the frozen image of Albert holding up his middle finger.

Hextor waved a fat slimy hand at the chairs in front of his desk. "Sit down. Put your feet up. Relax." He smiled sharp teeth and glared pointedly at Grace. "And tell me why you're not on that shit heap called Earth making my final fucking episode." He pointed to the wall of eyes showing Albert holding up his middle finger. "What the shit is that?"

Grace leaned over his desk. "I want you to guarantee season two."

His eyes flicked over her calmly, taking in her human appearance, and then lingering over Albert. "Nice move building up this one," he said, as though Albert wasn't there. "He's gained a smattering of the celebrity pull."

Albert shifted uncomfortably.

Hextor looked up at the ceiling as he spoke. "The Chook and Zojax love story... I suppose was okay. Exploiting Zojax's campaign and incorporating it into our show was genius. But now I've got the council sniffing my balls and advertisers pulling out."

He glanced back at the screens frozen with Albert and then looked directly at Grace. "This frozen monkey-fuck is making your ratings drop. Right when our show should be dropping a shit in the competition's mouth, so it's..." He shrugged. "Unfortunate. We might have to axe the show."

"But..." Her voice was soft. "I created this. It's mine."

"Yours?" He chuckled, looked her up and down then screamed, "THEY'RE ALL MY FUCKING SHOWS. Every one we make is mine." He paused, patted his sweaty baldhead and gestured to the chairs in front of his desk again. "Now, please, sit the fuck down."

Hesitantly, Grace sat. Albert did also.

"Sweetheart, I'm not going to tell you how to spread your cheese. But I want my final episode and you need to step it up!" He leaned forward, looking into her eyes conspiratorially. "I will give you a few pointers. First, you could go back and get super funky with your little love interest" – he smiled at Albert, leering over his body – "and have his dirty love child. That'll pop the viewers' distractions."

Albert felt a whirlpool of discomfort spinning in his gut. He didn't want to be involved in this. And was it even possible for their two species to mate?

"But it had better be a truly magical moment that tickles my slippery balls because I want more viewers. I want controversy."

Grace nodded. Albert felt sick.

"In fact, give me a fucking war on their whole planet. People will tune in for that. Fuck me. Even I'd watch five minutes of the monkeys slaying each other."

"But humans are intelligent living beings." Albert said.

Hextor glared at him and screwed up his face, then said in a soft mocking voice. *"But the humans are living beings."* He laughed. "Fuck off!"

Grace shook her head. "The council won't allow me to kill an intelligent species."

"Intelligent?" he scoffed. "If it gets me numbers, I don't care."

"This is so wrong." Albert shook his head. He needed to stop this. End this. This couldn't be allowed to go on any further.

Hextor leaned back with his hands behind his head. "Little Grace, do you want to step into the big pond? Or" – he looked pointedly at Albert –"keep swimming with the pissy tadpoles?"

She eyed Hextor. "I'm ready for the big pond."

Albert looked at her.

"Do you like lots of juicy money?" Hextor asked. "Expensive things?"

She shrugged. "Who doesn't?"

"Well then." He stood out of his chair and began to move in

what looked like a dance, bopping up and down. "You'll understand this."

"I think I do," she said, watching him with raised eyebrows.

Hextor gyrated his hips to some silent rhythm. Albert had no idea what the alien was doing. The large grotesque frog was bopping, dressed in his fancy suit, gazing at him with what he could only guess were meant to be sexy eyes, making thrusts with his pelvis.

"Grace, you need to start thinking with your big dick."

Incredulity dripped from her voice. "You want me to think with a penis?"

"Yeah." Hextor continued dancing, thrusting toward Albert.

Albert glanced around the room feeling extremely uncomfortable. The large alien's crotch came back and forth near his face. If this fat frog tried anything, Albert would... He didn't know. How could he escape? He was on an alien spaceship.

"Think big dick." Hextor's crotch was at Albert's eye level. "I know you don't have one like me, but the real big dick happens up here." Looking at Grace, he tapped the side of his forehead. "Use your mental dick. Imagine your finale is huge." Then he closed his eyes and sung. "*Make it number one.*" He thrust his crotch hard. "Now, Grace, stand up. Dance with me."

She looked across at Albert with concern and said to Hextor, "No, I'm alright. I get it. Think big, right?"

"You want season two. You fucking dance."

"Sorry," she whispered to Albert and slowly rose from her seat. She made an awkward little bop up and down.

"Now thrust your dick at him."

Grace made a small pelvic motion.

"Do it harder."

"Like this?" She was rocking her hips back and forth. She smiled apologetically at Albert.

"Visualise your big fucking ending." Hextor thrust harder. "Make it." He thrust. "Massive." Thrust. "Fuck those monkeys."

Albert watched them thrust towards him, feeling humiliated.

Feeling angry. This highly advanced alien civilisation was just as crass and stupid as his. Was the universe run by idiots?

Grace thrust back and forth rapidly near Albert's face.

"Enough!" Albert yelled. "I won't take this anymore!" He stood up with rage in his eyes. "You Gatogrosians are cruel and awful. This isn't how the universe is meant to be."

Hextor smiled. "Seems your little monkey does have some backbone."

Albert wanted to spit on him, attack him, or possibly slap the alien in the ear if he had one, but instead said, "You sir are an embarrassment to evolution."

Hextor shrugged and sat down. His green chin wobbled as he spoke, "Now Grace, how are you going make my magic? I want that final episode to start with a bang."

"It already has." Grace smiled slyly and nodded at the wall of eyes. "You're on it."

The eyeball screens blinked. Each showed different angles of the three of them in Hextor's office.

"Fuck," said Hextor and Albert in unison.

22

BOBBY-AS-ALBERT STAGGERED out of the glowing doorway and held a hand against his belly. The aftermath of being flung apart and re-smooshed together wasn't getting any easier. Nausea washed through his gut and he breathed deep to suppress the urge to vomit.

As his eyes adjusted in the pulsating blue glow of the door, Bobby saw only darkness. He stumbled to the edge of the black and tapped the ground with his shoe. It was hard as concrete. He couldn't see anything beyond. No stars, just black, like an abyss.

"Hello?" he called. "Anybody out there?"

Chook came lurching through behind him, also gripping his stomach and groaning.

The doorway hissed and vanished. Pure darkness fell upon them, so thick it swallowed them. Bobby couldn't see his fingers.

A loud gong rang out. Its heavy bass reverberated in Bobby's bones.

"I don't like this," Chook said. "I wanna go home."

Then fierce bright beams shone down as though they stood under searchlights, blinding them. Chook shielded his face. Then they heard a deafening roar. A gargantuan crowd screamed and clapped. Bobby held his hand up, squinting and trying to see behind the light. Slowly as his eyes adjusted and the ambient light came up he saw they were on one side of a vast arena, surrounded by a crowd of millions, all yelling and screaming. On one side, aliens waved banners of the circle surrounding a fist. The sound was extreme, louder than a jet engine or a volcano exploding – almost as loud as a football match.

"Oh shit," said Chook.

"We have to get out of here."

Above them, a massive eyeball floated high over the stadium, so much bigger than the ones back home, in the way the sun was bigger than Earth. Its iris frosted over, showing two glamorous aliens sitting on a couch, peering down.

"Ladies, gentlemen and beautiful non-binaries," one frog said. "Tonight, we're serving up a lovely meal of gnarly death."

"Look, Blax." The other one clapped. "The monkeys have arrived." It waved. "Hello, Bertie-man. Are you ready to die?"

Bobby-as-Albert saluted his middle finger at the eye and screamed, "Fuck off."

The crowd cheered, loving it.

"Drixilio, there's his signature move. Perhaps we should call him the Alpha-Bertie."

"I give him three minutes tops."

On the other side of the arena, a blue doorway flickered into existence.

"Quick!" said Chook. "There's our way out." He began to sprint towards the doorway.

Bobby followed, his feet pounding on the hard dirt floor. This was fucked, so fucked.

Out of the doorway jumped several soldiers. They had long thick tails coming out of their backsides. Their angular heads lacked noses and they had eyes on the sides of their heads. They looked like tall geckos, holding guns. As soon as they saw Bobby and Chook running towards them, they turned invisible. Then flashes of gunfire erupted from their direction. Bullets ricocheted off the ground, spitting up puffs of dust.

Bobby and Chook dived behind a boulder.

The crowd roared.

Bobby slapped the button on his clear-eye suit and vanished.

"Don't leave me," Chook said, hitting the button on his suit too.

They looked at each other in their pink translucent form.

"Well, folks." Blax grinned his pointy teeth high on the screen above. "Tonight, it's monkeys versus lizards."

The geckos re-materialised into solid form, held up their guns to the roaring crowd and fired. Their bullets fizzed flashing light as they hit a barrier protecting the crowd.

Shit, shit, thought Bobby as he crouched low. They could get out of this. Come on, think.

More gunfire sounded. Bullets bounced off the top of the boulder. It would only be a minute before those geckos were on them.

Blax said, "Our cheeky lizards might have an early win this—"

Gunshots boomed throughout the stadium and Blax vanished from the floating eye's screen. It oozed white jelly out of bullet size punctures, dropping splatters of gloop as it slowly deflated and descended towards the dirt with a fizz.

Bullets bounced off the boulder. The eye crashed with a heavy splat.

Chook, tugged out his vaporiser. "I don't want to die. I'm too young."

"Not dead yet."

Bullets whizzed overhead.

Bobby's invisibility suit glitched back into vision. Fuck, fuck, fuck. He slapped at the chest button. Not again. Slap. His hand, arms, torso, everything was visible.

Chook stared at him with concern. "Still feeling confident?"

The crowd roared.

Bobby crouched low. There had to be a way. There had to be something. He rubbed his chin thinking. His chin was very stubbly. It wasn't chin he remembered. That's it.

"Fucking gold," he said to Chook. "We're going to survive. Give me Zojax's transmorpher."

"Just for the record" - Chook tugged it out and passed it over – "every plan you've suggested since this stupid journey began has sucked."

"Happy to listen to yours."

Chook considered this for a moment before he pressed the vape to his lips. He exhaled a cloud and raised one eyebrow at him as bullets bounced above. "The Albert body suits you. You look like an idiot."

The gunfire eased and the crowd became quiet. It reminded Bobby of the solemn moment he'd heard of in history class, the moment before World War One soldiers climbed out of the trenches and charged.

"I'm going to use the transmorpher to turn you into a lizard. Then I'll get us some guns."

Chook looked back and forth between the device in Bobby's hand and Bobby's face. "Why should I be the one who transforms into a lizard?"

"Because you're better at speaking to aliens. You fell in love with one."

Chook huffed and crossed his arms. "So how will you get the guns?"

Bobby tried to smile genuinely. "With your invisibility suit 'cos mine is broken."

"No. And just no. Your idea is so shit. That's never going to happen."

More bullets. Dirt showered them.

"Fine," said Bobby. "You can get the guns. But first, see if you can get me a pic of one of those lizard freaks."

Chook hit his chest, turned invisible and edged up to the top of the boulder to peer over. Bobby placed the vape on his lips and sucked a jet of warm scented smoke into his lungs. The familiar sense in his brain unlocked.

Chook snapped a photo with his phone and slid down. "Two

are visible and another four are closing in."

"Let's assume they can't see you when you're invisible, because they didn't shoot us before."

Chook nodded and handed him his phone. Bobby synced the photo with the silver transmorpher, waited for a green light to appear, and handed it to Chook. "Do it."

Holding it against Bobby's temple, Chook asked, "Are you ready?"

"Not even remotely."

The button clicked. Bobby cried out as his body stretched and morphed. More bullets bounced off the top of the boulder. Bobby's skin changed from Albert's to a rock-coloured grey as scales formed, his nose melded with his face and stretched long like a lizard's. His eyes stretched further apart, and became wider and bigger on the side of his head. Bobby yelped in pain, but his yelps became deeper and more guttural.

Lizard Bobby lay on the ground, panting and realised that if this didn't work, it might be the last time they ever spoke. "Chook," Bobby said. "Brother, you've been the best friend anyone could ever hope for."

"Don't get sentimental. I'll be back here in no time to complain about you."

"I love your complaining."

"Okay, you're being weird. I should go."

Bobby watched Chook's pink body run out into the field. Good luck, he thought. Then Bobby stood, testing his balance in his new lizard body, and checked out his clawed hands. Awesome.

Two gecko soldiers stepped around the side of the boulder, pointing their guns at him. Seeing Lizard Bobby, they stopped.

One gecko looked at him sidelong. Its tongue flicked across one eye. "Louis, is that you?"

Fuck! Bobby thought. I can understand them. I thought that gloop shit would've worn off by now.

"No, no," said the other gecko. "I'm Louis. That's Alan. My

snout is more pronounced." The lizard leaned forward. "Alan, where is the monkey you were meant to kill?"

"Bro, relax." Bobby gesticulated widely with his clawed hand, thinking, Chook, where the fuck are you? Now would be a good time. "Let just chill out."

The lizards looked sideways at each other. "Whatever he said sounded like 'ooga booga'."

"You cannot say that." The other shook his head. "Alan has a speech disability."

"A lisp isn't a disability. And he clearly wasn't lisping."

The first lizard turned its head side on so one eye looked directly at Bobby. Its tongue flicked over its eyeball. "Alan? Tell us again. Slowly."

Both geckos exploded into chunks of meat and Bobby dived behind the boulder.

"Die, fucking lizards," Chook shouted as he continued to fire.

The noise was deafening. Bobby peered around the rock and saw pieces of gecko – limbs, torsos, heads – bouncing across the ground as bullets punctured them.

"Chook!" Bobby shouted. "Stop shooting." He stepped out from behind the boulder. "They're dead."

Chook turned, still shooting and pain exploded in Bobby's leg like a thousand knives stabbing his thigh. Blood splattered everywhere. "Fuck, Chook! " he screamed, hitting the dirt. "It's me."

Chook dropped to his knees, holding his smoking gun, tears in his eyes and his face looking as if he'd swallowed a lemon. "Bobby... I didn't mean... I was just trying... Sorry."

Bobby gritted his teeth and rolled face first into the dirt as agony ripped through him.

23

IN HEXTOR'S office Albert watched the wall of eyes showing Bobby and Chook. Those boys better survive.

Grace was at the back of the room on her phone making some deal, but Albert dare not look away from the screens. Each eyeball displayed a different angle or close-up. As bullets bounced off the top of the boulder, dirt showered onto Bobby's lizard face as he writhed in pain clinging to his bloody leg. Squatting next to him was a pink semi-transparent Chook, holding a weapon close. Chook glanced nervously from Bobby to the boulder's edge. Another wide shot showed the last three lizards creeping towards them.

Grace came back and sat in her chair.

Hextor said to Grace in a soft voice, "Using us to start the episode was quite clever. Well done. This ending could trump all endings. Death rates better than sex."

"It's not over yet," Grace said, patting the glass phone in her lap. Her eyes flicked back and forth between the screens as she sipped at her glowing drink. "They might survive. And I have just organised a lovely surprise."

Albert noticed she seemed very calm, very businesslike.

"Fuck those monkeys." Hextor sipped his glick while he leered at Grace's chest. "Make them suffer," he whispered to her. "Turn them into meat carcasses. And do it in a way that stiffens my ramrod" – he nodded at his crotch – "or you're out on your arse. No season two." He clicked his fingers and blew out a stream of air as if he were blowing out a candle.

She frowned at him and stepped further away.

Could this be happening? Albert thought, watching the screen.

The lizards were advancing, firing at the boulder.

"You gotta get out of here," Bobby said. "I'll cover you."

When the lizard's bullets stopped Bobby jumped up, wincing in pain as he aimed with one eye closed, then returned a volley of bullets. The gun shuddered in his arms with a deafening sound. The pink translucent form of Chook then bolted onto the battlefield. As Bobby's gun hammered at the lizards, Chook ducked and weaved, constantly changing his position, trying to get behind the geckoes.

Perspiration beaded on Albert's forehead. The boys' odds weren't great, but they'd already taken out three lizards.

Hextor took another step towards Grace. "They better not survive."

She took another step away.

On the screen, Bobby and Chook gunned down the last lizards and high-fived.

Hextor leered. "The only happy ending I want is one where I'm on top." He tugged at his collar. "Do you think it's hot in here?" He began to unbutton his shirt. "Maybe we should get more comfortable."

Grace glared at him. "Stop acting like a sex offender."

"A Gatogrosian can look at something delicious."

Grace took a deep breath and said, "Never going to happen, Hextor." She returned her attention to the eyeballs. "Fuck off."

He looked at Albert. "What about you monkey-man, wanna get naked with me?"

"No." Albert swallowed and stared harder at the screen. At the other end of the arena, another blue doorway appeared and out jumped six three-foot-high creatures with brown matted fur and rabbit ears, holding guns almost as big as themselves.

"Bunnies," Bobby and Chook said.

The bunnies immediately vanished from sight but flashes from their gun barrels could be seen as Bobby and Chook crouched low.

"We need a diversion," Bobby said.

Hextor reached out and touched Grace, his hand running up her arm. "I know you want to go further in this industry."

"Hey, hey, hey," Albert said, stepping forward. "Leave her alone."

"Albert, I don't need you to do that. I've got this." Grace turned to Hextor. "Fuck off."

He smiled. "Tickle my slippery balls and" – his little tongue darted across his green lips – "your career will soar." Perspiration glistened off his forehead, and he flicked back his stringy green hair with his free hand. "Taste of my sweet delights." He ran his hand over her shoulder and down her back.

Grace stepped away again.

"Fine, you're fired."

"Hextor, if you've taught me anything, it's only the ratings that matter."

Right then, an electric hum filled the room, wind blew and a glowing blue doorway appeared. Several armed uniformed Gatogrosians stepped through and formed a perimeter around the doorway.

Hextor looked around wildly. "Fuck. Council guards."

Albert felt nervous.

Grace took a calm sip from her glass.

A frog in a white smock like Blixitor's stepped through the doorway. "The council is revoking your licence."

Hextor glared at Grace with hate. "You did this for those pathetic monkeys?"

Grace nodded at the screens. They had changed to broadcast what had occurred minutes before. *"Tickle my slippery balls and your career will soar."*

"They might be replaying this episode for a while," said Grace.

24

BOBBY'S LIZARD leg was still bleeding. "Chook," he said. "We need a plan."

Chook kept firing madly at the bunnies until his gun clicked. He tried it again. Click. "I'm out of bullets."

"Take mine," said Bobby, holding out his gun.

Chook grabbed it, popped his head over the boulder and began firing.

Bobby gritted his lizard teeth through the pain. Maybe they would get through this. Maybe they would return home and see their friends and family again, he thought, watching Chook return fire. He was awesome at this.

Then Bobby's gun began to click.

"Shit," said Chook, sliding down.

Return gunfire continued to bounce off the boulder. Bobby held onto his leg. Searing pain bit into him. He didn't want to tell Chook, but it would only be a matter of moments before those rabbits realised they couldn't shoot back.

Chook cocked his head like a puppy listening. "You hear that?"

Bobby strained his ear holes against the cacophony of gun

blasts, and there, below the noise, he heard the familiar electrical hum of a doorway materialising.

It flashed and fizzled into existence before them, pulsating with blue light.

The rabbits fired their guns towards it, but their bullets vanished into the light. Out of the doorway came a glowing green force field. The gunfire bounced off it. Then behind it stepped out a very handsome frog-man holding a very large gun, dressed in black fatigues that sported the symbol of a circle around a red fist.

"Zojax!" Chook shouted. "You came back!"

Zojax gave Chook a wink before holding up his gun and proceeding to take down the bunnies, one by one.

The crowd roared with delight.

Zojax held out his arms to Chook. "Come give me some sweet love, baby."

"You're lucky I don't have any bullets."

Zojax placed a hand on Chook's shoulder. "I wouldn't abandon you."

"Really?" Chook looked up into his green eyes. "You certainly seemed to."

"Chooky. Honestly." Zojax embraced him. "Now plant your candy lips here."

Amidst the smoke and death, Chook and Zojax pressed their lips together.

"Seriously!" said Bobby, crouching low. "There'll be time for that later. Let's get out of here."

"Good to see you too, Bobby." Zojax smiled, letting go of Chook. "I'm sorry I—"

"It's cool. Let's just go," said Bobby, limping as blood poured down his lizard leg.

Zojax and Chook held hands, then leapt into the doorway. Bobby hobbled up the doorway, turned to the crowd and saluted them with his middle finger, and then jumped. For the second time that day felt himself being stretched into an atomic smear across the universe.

Bobby leaned back into Zojax's couch happy to have his body returned. The sofa's weird moss felt warm and soft, which was perfect because every muscle hurt, muscles he didn't know he had. He stretched out his leg, probing it with his finger. Despite it being repaired by travelling through the doorway, he expected it to feel tender. "Cool if we crash here for a while?" He stretched out his arms looking at the wall tattoos. "I'm not ready to head back to Earth."

Zojax smiled from another couch across the room. "My home is your home."

The frog-man and Chook were sitting close on another couch, while Chook was listening to his gran on the Zojax's phone. "Yes, I know, I did say I wouldn't travel very far again. And technically I haven't. I only went through one doorway." Chook held out his vaporiser for Bobby.

Bobby shook his head and whispered, "I'm going to stay clear-headed for a while. I've got a lot to process. "

Chook raised one eyebrow and returned to his conversation on the phone. "You say the pink eyes are all gone. Gran, that's great... What? No! Those ladies at your bridge group shouldn't want them back. It's not boring now, it's normal."

Bobby let his eyes slip shut. This had been a mad ride, and not just that last jump through the doorway. From the very beginning.

"Yes, I love you too," Chook said. "No, I don't know when I'll be home. Okay. Love you." Chook handed the phone back to Zojax and snuggled close. After a moment he said into Zojax chest. "I thought we were going to die in that arena. And when I got hold of the gun... I'm not sure what came over me"

Zojax whispered. "You did what you had to, sweetie."

"And I'm glad you did," said Bobby.

Chook looked across at Bobby and said, "Gran thinks everything back home has settled down. Like nothing ever happened and we're probably not even in trouble anymore."

"Maybe. Maybe not." Bobby nodded and looked out the window. "I don't believe it or" – he paused – "I'm not ready to. I need to know one hundred per cent those pink eyes are gone." From here the stars all looked different. Somewhere out there was Earth and everyone he knew – his mum, Kitty, Baz, old Bill. He'd never been away from home this long before and his mum would probably be losing the plot with worry. "Zojax, could I use your phone too?"

Before he could answer, a chime rang through the room. It sounded like the tinkling of rain on a xylophone.

"Hang on." Zojax extracted himself from Chook and the couch and walked to the door.

"Wait!" said Bobby. His body began to tense. "Don't answer it. They could be coming to arrest us."

"Relax. No one ever got arrested for being on a TV show." Zojax swung open the door.

A slender, glamorous frog-lady stepped into the room, followed by Albert. She wore a smart-fitting sparkly suit and her green hair was styled in a pixie cut. Her eyes shone like she knew a joke that you didn't.

"Ms Jacobs! Albert!" Bobby said in surprise. Then he narrowed his eyes. "Why are you here?"

"Albert's going to stay here with you." Ms Jacobs grinned sharp teeth. "For season two."

Bobby wanted to tell her to shove her show up her arse, but one thing he'd learned from the space bar was that sometimes it's better to keep your thoughts to yourself.

"You guys have taken the universe by storm. Every talk show in the three sectors wants an interview with you. We must capitalise on this."

Bobby tried to get up from the window. There is no way in hell he was going to work for her.

"Why would we?" Zojax beat him to it.

"Lots more primitive cultures are still being exploited. They need your help." She smiled and winked at Zojax. "They need us to save them."

"You're going to make shows about this?"

Grace nodded. "Isn't it fabulous?"

"Making money off exploitation but calling it a rescue is even more messed up. Why can't you just leave them alone?"

Grace patted Albert's hand. "You and the boys take some time to think about it. It's been a very tiring couple of days." Then, in a low voice, she said looking at Bobby "I'm pretty sure you'll be pleased about being paid this time."

Grace left and Albert stayed, plonking himself next to Bobby on the moss sofa.

"What the fuck is wrong with her?"

Albert shrugged, looking out the window. "Listen, Bobby. I am sorry about any trouble I caused you."

Bobby watched at him gazing at the stars. He had hated Albert, punched him, mocked him – hell, he'd even worn t-shirts with Albert's face on them. And Bobby had done all that without really knowing who Albert was. And now, apparently they were all well known faces throughout the universe. "Albert, what's it like being famous?"

"Terrible. Or it was for me." Albert glanced back at Bobby from the stars. "I thought I wanted it, but really I wouldn't wish it on anyone. I know now that I'd prefer to quietly study the cosmos. And" – he looked back out the window – "I think, maybe, I might be able to do that here."

Bobby pointed at the stars. "So which one is our little rock?"

Albert smiled. "It's a little hard to work out because everything has moved around. But we're in the Pictor constellation. The one that's in the shape of an easel."

Bobby looked at him with a blank expression. "They all look like stars."

Albert laughed. "I imagine this is how my dad had felt when he showed me the stars."

Bobby swallowed. He couldn't even remember his dad.

Albert held up his hand and pointed. "Over there is Orion's arm." Bobby followed his finger. "See the yellowish star on the edge, in that sea of space?" Albert said. "That's our sun, Sol. Right next to it is Earth. About forty-two light-years away."

"Seems like we're far enough away to be out of trouble."

Albert shifted uncomfortably in his seat and then reached down and tugged something out from underneath him. "Is this a potato?"

ACKNOWLEDGMENTS

Wow! If you've gotten to this point without your brain melting, I'll take that as a win. Thanks for reading Pink Eye. I loved writing it so I really hope you enjoyed it.

And yes, I would love you to write a review. I know, I sound like another needy writer, but we live and die by our reviews. And honestly, I want to live. So write a good one. Nah, I'm joking, write an honest one. Praise me or execute me, the choice is yours. I read all of them, the painful and lovely, because they're all helpful. But please, please, please, write a good one.

And to all the people who helped me write this, thank you.

Because anyone who's ever completed a creative project knows a gazillion people helped them. And these wonderful folk encouraged me to believe in Pink Eye. They offered their wisdom, feedback and lots of cheeky comments to get this novel out of my brain and into reality.

A huge thanks to my family. You're all extremely supportive. Sandy, you're a rockstar. I'm the world's luckiest husband. Razzia and Corbin - thanks for being super encouraging, and great kids. Extra thanks to Corbin – the world's youngest beta reader at age 10 (yes, I know you're now 11).

Beta readers, Beth Clapton, Andrea Fogarty, Erik Hamre, Philip Wolf, and Michael Braithwaite thank you for your wonderful (and brutal) honesty. I love your astute eyeballs.

My excellent writers' group friends - Brett Savill, Erik Hamre, Peter Ninnes, Gary Fishlock, Mara Tisci, David Staume, Roger Patulny, Sophie Patulny, Triona Crowley, Jesse Hawley, Beth Clapton, and Karen Vega, thank you for your continuous dedication. Your support has kept me on task and out of the pub (mostly).

Simone Ford and Lauren Finger, thank you for being two of Australia's greatest editors and for taking my novel seriously. Your professional help has made Pink Eye so much better.

Rauri Rochford, thank you for happily answering my endless tech questions.

Professor Jonathon (Joss) Bland-Hawthorn, thank you for generously attempting to explain astrophysics. Your brain is amazing and rammed with ideas. Sorry if I wrote any science-ish bollocks, I tried to keep it real, but a little nonsense certainly lubricates the storytelling.

And special thanks to Doctor George Hobbs, who works at Parkes Radio Telescope and SETI, for happily explaining in detail how things work there. You are nothing like Albert. You are a brilliant, sincere, and true gentleman. Thank you for taking the time to answer my questions. And again, sorry about everything I got wrong.

WHO IS TOM NORTON?

Tom lives in a tiny terrace house in Sydney, Australia with his beautiful family and little cat. By day, he works as a TV editor on some of Australia's and the USA's biggest TV shows. He's also the co-host of a funny science podcast called Big Questions from Small Minds, where he talks to science professors with rather large brains.

Find out more about Tom and his upcoming books at tomnorton.au